THE RECRUIT

FINAL KINGDOM BOOK TWO

STEVEN K. SMITH

MB3 PRESS

MyBoys3 Press

Editing by: Kim Sheard (anotherviewediting.com)

Proofreading by: Stephanie Parent (polgarusstudio.com)

Book Cover Design by www.ebooklaunch.com

For more information, contact us at:

MyBoys3 Press, P.O. Box 2555, Midlothian, VA 23113

www.myboys3.com

Second Printing

ISBN: 978-1-947881-09-9

To Ryan,
Blazing a trail with the top down

THE RECRUIT

CHAPTER ONE_

I stared into the lens.

Across the digital bridge. Into the ether, through time and space.

"Hey, Zach. Yes, it's really me. I'm sorry for the theatrics, but I had to put that passcode on there to be sure only you could access this. You must be wondering what's happening. I don't blame you, and I'm sorry if this is scaring you, but it's the only way I can reach you now."

There was so much I could say, I barely knew where to start despite rehearsing it in my mind a dozen times. Keep it simple. There would be time for explanations later. Right now I had to warn him.

"I'm so sorry for disappearing. Mom and Dad must be freaked right about now. You have to believe me, I never meant for any of this to happen. I tried to hide, to fix things myself, but it's too late now. I never wanted to involve you in this, but I have to warn you. They're coming."

I paused, clenching my jaw to keep from breaking down. I

didn't want to say what came next, but I had to. It was the truth.

"I don't know if I can get back home, Zach. It might not be possible. I need you to say goodbye for me. Tell Mom and Dad I'm sorry, that I love them. And tell Maggie she will always be in my heart. But she has to remember my promise necklace. You have to take the code to Dr. William Hendrickson. He's a computer science professor at Tech. I've been working with his assistant Tyler Barnes. The password will give them access to the server where I copied everything they need to complete the JOSHUA machine. There's not enough time to explain, but I crossed into the digital realm, Zach. I had to hide. I'm here, inside *Kingdom*."

The drums were beating again. I had to keep moving. They were coming.

"Zach, you have to watch your back. You're not safe there. Find Dr. Hendrickson. Tell him the quantum accelerators are too hot. He has to use the data in the encrypted server that's accessed with the passcode on Maggie's promise necklace. He'll know what to do. Just be careful, brother. This isn't a game any longer. It's all too real."

SIX MONTHS EARLIER

"Bryce, why are you just standing there? Cross the river!"

I shook my head. "Patience. Not yet."

Zach grunted with annoyance. Patience was not one of my younger brother's strongest traits. He always wanted to hurtle forward through *Final Kingdom* with guns blazing. I'd been the same at his age, I supposed. Of course, *Kingdom* hadn't been released yet when I was in middle school, but I'd played hundreds of rounds in other adventure sagas. Even now, with plenty to fill my time, it was still fun to play a game like this. And it was flattering to know that my little brother wanted to spend time with me. So when he asked me to play after I'd come home from a run, it was easy to say yes.

My avatar stood on the side of the raging river as my thumb rested lightly on the edge of my controller. I waited for the water to recede to a passable level, even as the team of Rangers charged toward me over the ridge. I knew if I moved too soon, the current would sweep me downriver.

"Now!" I shouted when I saw the first rock break through the water line. My on-screen avatar surged ahead, splashing through the rapids and successfully leaping to the far bank. Trumpets sounded and a torrent of confetti rained down across the screen.

Level Completed.

Zach turned to me with his eyebrows raised. "How do you always know how to do that?"

I laughed and pulled off my gaming headset. "You can't hold back talent, little brother. It always rises to the top."

Zach frowned. "Whatever. I know luck when I see it."

I stopped in his doorway, turning on my heel. "Oh, should we play again? I didn't think you wanted me to wipe the floor with your sorry performance again. But if you want to..." I pretended to reach for my controller until Zach waved me off.

"Shut up. Just forget it. I gotta start my homework."

I nodded, wishing for a moment that I could be back doing middle-school-level work instead of studying for my AP Calculus final during this last week of school. My GPA needed to keep me near the top of my class if I wanted to get into Tech next fall. "Algebra?"

Zach shook his head. "Science. Physical properties."

"Newton's laws?"

"Maybe. It's boring."

"Boring? I love that stuff. Do you need help?"

"I've had enough of your help for one afternoon," said Zach. "But thanks."

A buzz sounded from the dresser. I reached for my phone, but Zach swiped it first.

"Guess who!" he teased.

"Is it Mags?"

"Maybe."

"Give it to me."

He turned and walked to his window. "Let's see what she has to say here. 'Oh, Bryce, you're so amazing. I miss you so much!'" He pretended to kiss the phone dramatically.

"Very funny." I pushed his arm down and grabbed the phone. "You're just jealous."

"Maybe."

I glanced at the screen and saw a text from Maggie.

Are you close?

I scrunched my eyebrows. Close? What did she mean? Then I yelled, suddenly remembering I'd asked her out for dinner tonight.

Martorano's at 6:30? Remember?? She texted back as if she'd heard me.

"Just go talk to her, will you, lover boy?" Zach shoved me into the hall and closed the door.

I bolted into the bathroom and flipped on the shower, pulling off my running clothes as I typed back.

Running late. Be there soon. Sorry.

CHAPTER TWO_

I spotted Maggie from the parking lot. She was in the booth by the window, but she didn't see me running in. I felt bad being late, but thankfully Martorano's was just down the road. It was the town of Milton's best Italian place—actually, it may have been the only Italian place—and they had the best calzones I'd ever tasted.

I nodded at the hostess, a girl I knew from school, and hurried over to Maggie.

"Hey, sorry I'm late." I bent over and gave her a quick kiss before sinking into the cushioned booth across from her to catch my breath. She was still wearing her nametag from the boutique she worked at after school on the days when she didn't have soccer practice.

"Did you come right from work..." I paused and stared at her tag. "Maggie?"

"How'd you guess?"

I smiled, hoping to lighten the mood. "I'm extremely intelligent."

"Uh-huh. Then maybe you can read a clock."

Ouch. Maybe I wasn't out of the doghouse yet.

Maggie glanced at my head. "Were you swimming?" She smirked at me and then took a long swig of her drink.

"Swimming?" I ran my fingers through my still wet hair. "Oh. No, I just came back from a run and had to shower. I figured late was better than sweaty."

She peered at me over her glass with her dark brown eyes that sometimes seemed as big as Frisbees. Knowing that those looks meant she liked me, maybe even loved me, always sent my stomach into butterflies. I resisted the urge to lean across the table and kiss her again.

The waitress, an older woman with orange hair, stepped up to our table. I'd never seen her there before, but *her* nametag said "Janice."

"You kids ready, or do you need more time?"

"Um…" I hesitated playfully, even though we both knew I always got a calzone. "I think I'm ready." I shot a glance across the table. "Unless you need more time."

Maggie rolled her eyes. "No, I've had more than enough time with the menu. I'll have the mushroom risotto with a house salad."

Janice jotted furiously on her order pad. "What kinda dressing you want, honey?"

"I'll have the raspberry vinaigrette, but can I get that on the side?" Maggie answered. "And can you hold the onions?"

Janice could have been writing a novel with the amount she'd scribbled on her little pad, but she eventually bounced her head back toward me. "And for you?"

"I'll just have the ham calzone. And can I get extra sauce for that?"

"On the side?" she asked.

"Sure. And can you hold the onions for me too?"

Janice finally stopped her furious writing and raised her eyes, but Maggie jumped in. "He's just joking. Sorry."

I gave Janice a half smile. "I was late."

"Uh-huh." She turned and left without seeing to appreciate my humor. I looked at Mags and wondered if she really was still mad.

"What were you up to this afternoon?" she asked.

"Not much. Just hung with Zach."

She sighed.

"What?" I said, my voice raised an octave.

"I know you were playing *Kingdom*."

"*Kingdom*?"

Maggie frowned. "Stop. I mean, whatever. It just seems like you have other things you could be doing. Like showing up on time for dinner with your girlfriend."

I raised my eyebrows. "Shoot, is she here?" I ducked my head and pretended to scan the other tables.

"Oh my god, Bryce."

I sensed it was time to be serious. "What can I say? I enjoy hanging out with my little brother, and he wanted to play *Kingdom*. What's wrong with that? Would you rather I beat the snot out of him?"

"No." Maggie sighed. "It's fine, I guess."

Dinner with Maggie trumped any video game with Zach, but the days when video games were just for kids were long gone. Today's graphics were on par with what the military used for their training exercises, and the sophisticated plotlines of many games were better than the latest Hollywood blockbusters.

"Do you know what I heard from Dan other day?" I asked, not quite ready to let it go.

She glanced at her phone. "Is this about video games?"

"No, it's about college."

College was a safe topic of conversation with Mags. It was practically all she and anyone else at school wanted to talk about these days. It was the same at home, where Mom and Dad were silently losing sleep over how they would pay for it. They tried not to add pressure, but I knew I needed a scholarship. My guidance counselor said I was a lock to get one from Tech, but you never knew until it happened.

Maggie set her phone on the table and looked back at me. "Dan Colton? Isn't he failing all his classes? What would he have to say about college?"

"I don't know about *his* grades," I said, "but his brother was home last weekend from *college*."

"Where'd he go? MCC?"

"No, somewhere in New England, I think." I really had no idea where Dan's brother went to school, but I was pretty sure it wasn't Milton's local community college. I stared back at her impatiently. "Can I finish? This is not the story I'm trying to tell."

"Sorry."

"So, Dan's brother comes home and says that the dorms are filled with guys who are constantly missing classes. And not just the struggling students, it's some of the top performers in the school."

"Why? Are they sick?"

"No, they're staying up way too late and not waking up in time for class."

Maggie shook her head. "They really shouldn't party that

hard. I mean, I love to have fun too, but don't they realize they're in school to learn?"

"No, that used to be the problem, but recently they're staying up all night gaming."

Maggie closed her eyes. "Idiots."

"That's a little harsh." Even though I didn't plan on skipping classes at Tech, or wherever I ended up getting in, I could easily picture occasionally staying up all night playing rounds of *Kingdom*.

She pulled her phone back out. "I thought you said this wasn't about video games?"

"I said it was about college, and it is. They're vying for the top slots at gaming competitions with the hope that execs from top tech companies might scout them for internships."

Maggie just shook her head again. "I really don't understand that. If they're so smart, you'd think they could find a better way to get ahead than playing video games."

I shrugged. "It's addicting. What can I say?"

Janice stopped at our table with a jug of water and refilled Maggie's drink after setting a glass in front of me.

"Thanks," I said.

Maggie's face turned serious. "What you can say is that you see my point. All that gaming distracts from what's important." She leaned back in her seat and smiled. "Like me."

I laughed. She *did* have a point. "Well, it's hard to argue with that. But there's one more thing I need to tell you. I got a message from Tech this morning."

She leaned closer. "Really?"

I nodded. "But I'll warn you, it *does* have to do with computers. Are you sure you want to hear about it?"

Her eyes narrowed. "Tell me before I hurt you." Maggie's

feistiness was one of the things I loved about her. It also didn't hurt that she was hot, but she had an edge to her too.

"They invited me for an official visit to the computer science department. And they said I could meet with the track coach and watch an afternoon practice."

Maggie's smile lit up the booth. "That's so exciting!" She reached across the table and squeezed my hand. "Did you tell your parents?"

I nodded. "They were stoked. The email invited family too, so I think Mom and Dad both want to come, and we'll probably bring Zach." I shot her a quick smile. "We might have one more space in the car. You said you've been meaning to take a tour."

I could see her mind already churning through the details. Maggie was considering applying to Tech's English department. She wanted to teach at an elementary school.

"That would be fun."

"The only problem is it's next Friday, and I know we were supposed to go to the movies with Liv and Jordan."

Maggie waved her hand. "We can do that another time." She looked back at me, her eyes still beaming. "This is huge. They're going to love you." She squeezed my hand a little tighter. "I know I do."

CHAPTER THREE_

"I can't believe this place!" Zach looked at me wide-eyed. "Can I just skip high school and come here with you?"

I laughed and shook my head as we walked through one of Tech's freshman dorms. "Sorry. I'm afraid you have a few more years to wait, buddy." Our guide, Kyle, said the college calendar finished earlier in the year than high school. Spring semester had already ended, so many students were on summer break. But even without the full complement of students, the place seemed pretty killer.

"Are there any girls' floors in this building?" asked Maggie.

Kyle nodded. "Actually, this is a co-ed dorm, so all the floors are mixed."

Mom coughed nervously.

"But we have others that are strictly guys or girls," he added quickly.

Mom patted me on the shoulder. "I think one of those might be a better place to start, honey."

"Okay, Mother," I said, rolling my eyes. Kyle gave me an

"I know how parents are" kind of glance. He probably heard parents say that a lot when showing people around.

After visiting the dorm, we walked to a tall building that housed the computer science department. "This is Lightcap Hall," said Kyle. "It's one of our newest and most high-tech facilities. Not only is it a certified green building, but the optic cables running through the labs are of the same caliber as those used at Microsoft and Google."

That sounded exciting. I'd taken online programming classes from Stanford last semester. Stanford is in California, but Mom said online was as close to college on the West Coast as I was going to get. I hoped those classes would carry some serious weight on my college applications, and maybe even count as college credits.

I had a knack for coding. Maggie said it seemed like Chinese to her, but for me it was a lot like running. They both put me into a zone where everything seemed to flow naturally. With coding, instead of looking for the fastest path around the track, my brain seemed to instinctively find connections between the programming sequences.

Maybe it was why I loved playing *Kingdom.* It was like recreational programming. More than any other game I'd played, *Kingdom* challenged players to use logic and find the best path through the levels. When I was in the game, I felt like I was trying to outsmart the programmers as much as the other players. My friends were always saying I should work for a gaming company someday. Maybe even one like Q2, where I could design new levels to *Final Kingdom.* The news was full of stories about kids right out of school landing jobs with juicy comp packages at tech start-ups. Some of those companies quickly exploded and went public, turning the twenty-somethings into multi-millionaires overnight.

Getting rich wasn't my life's ambition, but I supposed it couldn't hurt. Ever since Dad had started his new job, my parents had been struggling to make ends meet. They didn't talk about it much, and they shielded me and Zach from most of it, but I wasn't blind. When I told Dad about my idea to develop software to help people in the developing world, he thought that was a great use of my skills. But he also advised me not to underestimate the importance of putting bread on the table for my future family.

We toured the main part of the computer building, meeting several professors and a graduate assistant. Everyone was very enthusiastic about the program and the quality of the instruction. They could have just been putting on a happy face for visitors, but you only had to look around the glittering new building to believe they were being honest. The labs were larger than anything we had back at Milton, and I could already feel my brain navigating through some of the equations posted on the boards. I'd hoped to meet the head of the department, but unfortunately he'd been called out of town for a special project.

Kyle left us in the lobby. Zach had been bugging Dad to show him the football stadium, and Mom offered to help Maggie find the English department. I told them I'd catch up. I felt a pull to stay a bit longer and wander around the building. It was enticing, picturing myself attending school there, learning advanced computing methods, and working on groundbreaking research that was hailed in prestigious journals around the world. Outside of Silicon Valley and maybe Cambridge, this was one of the hottest places in the world for a programmer. I tried to let that sink in as I wandered the hallways, my mind caught up in my daydreams.

I took the stairs to the bottom floor, following a small sign for a lab. Kyle had showed us several, but I was curious whether they were all the same. I stopped near the end of the hall in front of a glass door with "LAB" written across the pane. The lights were dimmed, but a steady electronic glow from the rows of computer terminals spread throughout the room.

Without thinking, I stepped inside, drawn toward a giant video board on the wall. It was unlike anything I'd ever seen—streams of code and computations flowed across the enormous board, seeming to move in real time.

"Look interesting?" a voice said from behind me.

I jumped away from the screen, suddenly self-conscious of having walked in uninvited. Maybe I wasn't supposed to be there. "Oh, sorry. I was just leaving."

The man who'd spoken was watching me curiously. "You were staring at those lines like they meant something to you. Do they?"

I hesitated, uncertain if I should say anything, but I couldn't help it. "I thought so, but now I'm not so sure."

"What did you think it was?"

I swallowed hard and went for it. What did I have to lose? "I thought it was a streaming algorithm. A dynamic sequence pathway. But I don't think I'm right."

"What would you do next?" the man replied. "Where would you take it from there?"

I stared back at the board and took a tentative step forward. "May I?"

"Have at it."

I studied the lines, following the polymorphic flows with my finger, tracing the logic statements through to their natural conclusions. I tried to see past the numbers—a trick I'd learned from an online TED Talk by a VP at Intel. He said some of their best programmers had an uncanny ability to see through the code, to cut through the clutter and see the picture it forms. It had made little sense at first, but the more I tried it, the more things started to come together in my brain. Now, when I was stuck on something in class, I tried to step back, allow my mind to wander, and let the answer come to me, like an ocean wave crashing onto the shore.

I stared deeper, studying the patterns in the code. "It might be a parallel cluster algorithm." I pointed to the highest line and tried to collect my thoughts. "If this thread is 'X,' then the recursion would be positive, meaning that the sequence must move this way, barring any mutations." I stepped back and felt my face flush. "I mean, I think so."

The man was watching me with his head half-cocked. "What did you say your name was?"

"Bryce. Bryce Pearson."

"Uh-huh. And you're a student here, Mr. Pearson?"

I chuckled, nervously. "No, just on a tour. I'm going to be a high school senior down in Milton. I'm hoping to come here though. Probably in CS, but I run track too, so I'm heading there after lunch."

"Track, huh?" the man said. "Sprints or distance?"

"Mostly the mile and the 400-meter relay."

"Professor Hendrickson, have you seen this message?" A younger man walked through the doorway from the hall. He stopped when he saw me standing in front of the board. "Oh. I'm sorry. I didn't know you were with someone."

"Hi, Sean," said the man. Professor Hendrickson. I racked my brain for how I knew that name.

I moved from the board. "I should be going. I need to catch up with my family."

Dr. Hendrickson extended his arm. I shook his hand, feeling a little awkward for having barged in and become engaged in whatever that little test was.

"Nice talking with you, Bryce."

"You too." I stopped in the doorway, trying to remember which way the elevator was. I looked back and they were both staring at me. It was weird.

CHAPTER FOUR_

I caught up with everyone at the student center in the middle of campus. There were ten times more choices for lunch than at Milton's cafeteria. Zach had two pieces of carrot cake, and he looked ready to eat my dessert as well. He seemed prepared to take my place at Tech in a heartbeat if only he were old enough.

"Did you meet any more professors?" asked Mom, who was sitting across from Maggie and me.

"Yeah," I said in between bites.

"What were their names?" asked Dad.

I shrugged and took another bite of cake. "I forget."

I'm not sure why I didn't tell them more. There was something secretive in how Professor Hendrickson had asked me questions and watched me work through the problem on the board. Like he was secretly evaluating me. He'd reacted like my answers were correct, which felt good, but something was off. My instincts said to keep the whole thing to myself for now.

"Did you see the English department?" I asked Maggie, trying to move the conversation along.

"I did. It was wonderful." She leaned closer to me and squeezed my arm. "It all just feels so right. You know what I mean?"

I nodded and stared through a wall of high windows which overlooked the grassy quad in the center of campus. It was easy to picture the two of us here. But any place out on my own seemed right, especially if Mags was there. I needed to get out of Milton. I loved Mom and Dad and Zach, but something tugged at my edges and said it was time to start my own life. Maybe everyone feels that way at some point. I was sure I'd miss home when I was gone, but the sensation grew stronger with each passing week.

"Ready to check out the athletic department?" asked Dad, as his cell phone rang in his pocket. He looked at the screen and frowned. "Sorry, this is work. I've got to take this." He stood and walked toward the exit.

Zach grabbed my arm. "Do you think we can run on the track?"

Maggie laughed. "I almost guarantee it, Zach."

Dad was sitting on a picnic table, still talking on the phone, when we walked out of the student center. He waved and motioned that he'd catch up. Mom sighed, but urged us on. "I'm sure he'll finish soon. I think it's Frank."

"Frank?" asked Maggie.

"Dad's new boss," explained Zach. "He calls a lot."

"He's trying to get his foot in the door there, honey," Mom said. "Sometimes that takes time. It's difficult starting a new job after working at a place as long as your father did."

Lurking in all of Tech's awesomeness was the inescapable fact it would cost a lot to attend a place like this. It wasn't in my parents' nature to say something was off the table, but I could tell that the prospect of paying for my schooling was weighing on them. Dad always spoke with pride about how he'd been the first in his family to go to college. He'd come from a long line of hard-working dairy farmers. For generations, farming had just been what you did when you grew up. Grandpa Pearson hadn't liked the idea of Dad leaving the farm, but Dad loved to talk about all the doors that his business degree had opened for him. I knew he wanted me to have the same opportunity.

The athletic center's indoor training facility was like something you would expect from a professional sports team. When our high school expanded, they converted the old auxiliary gym into one of the best training rooms in the county, but it paled in comparison to this place.

"Holy cow," whistled Zach, staring at the rows of shiny weight machines. Dozens of students were working out all around the room.

A pretty girl walked past us in tight shorts and a sports bra, but I did my best not to look. "Eyes straight ahead," said Maggie.

Zach chuckled and nudged me in the ribs. An adult trainer must have noticed us gawking at the facility from the doorway, because he waved us over. "Help you find something?"

I smiled and pointed to the turn of the indoor track that circled along the balcony above us. "I'm here to speak with Coach Robb."

The man nodded. "You're speaking to him."

"Hi, I'm Bryce Pearson." I extended my hand like Hendrickson had done back in the lab and tried to sound confident. "I'm hoping to run for you next year."

"On scholarship," chirped Zach.

I stared down at him and shook my head. "Quiet, Zach." I felt my face turning red.

Coach Robb just laughed. "Nice to meet you, Bryce." He looked over my shoulder. "And this must be your family?"

I nodded and introduced him to everyone, with Dad walking up as we finished. The coach toured us around the weight room and the track, then to the other side of the parking lot and the outdoor track.

"I've watched your race footage from the sectionals," said Coach Robb. "Your relay times are impressive."

Maggie smiled and I nodded with pride. Coach Simmons had told me he'd made a highlight reel of my best times and sent them to a few schools. It was good to hear someone had actually watched them.

"We've been searching for a solid men's relay anchor for a while." He pursed his lips, his eyes bouncing from me to Mom and Dad. "But I need to be honest with you. We're thin on scholarship slots this recruiting year. We'll only have two graduating seniors, so competition will be fierce."

I considered his words. I'd never been one for giving up even when the odds were against me. As long as there were open slots, I still had a chance. Dad shot me a look like I should say something.

I cleared my throat. "I'm a hard worker, Coach. I promise I won't let you down."

"He's real fast," added Zach. "Ask anybody. They'll tell you it's true."

Coach Robb laughed. "Well that's good to hear, both of you. I run a tight ship, but I'm fair, if you give me all you have." He turned to Zach and grinned. "You can ask anybody about *that,* too."

CHAPTER FIVE_

My mind buzzed the whole drive back from Tech. It was late, and Mags had fallen asleep on my shoulder. Zach was in the back row, texting on his phone with his friend Andrew. I was exhausted too, but I couldn't stop thinking through all I'd seen and heard. I could now imagine what it would be like attending college, taking classes, learning advanced programming from world-class professors, maybe even running anchor on the track team. With track scholarships thin next year, keeping my high school grades up was now even more important. An academic scholarship might be my best option.

I wondered where Professor Hendrickson fit into the scholarship decision process. He'd been aloof, but he'd seemed impressed by my work. Maybe I should send him a follow-up letter thanking him for letting me work through the problems on his board. It couldn't hurt. That seemed like a mature thing to do. Dad often said that if you act like you belong somewhere, others are more likely to see you that way too.

We dropped Maggie off on our way home. I grabbed a quick snack before heading to bed.

"Big day," said Dad, stopping in the kitchen.

"Yeah."

"Did you like what you saw?"

I nodded. "How could you not? It was amazing."

"College is a big change," said Dad. "Not just for you, but for your mother and me, and Zach, too. It'll be strange." He nudged me with his elbow. "We kind of like having you around."

I rolled my eyes. "It's only a couple hours away, Dad. And it's not like I'd be moving to the other side of the country."

"I know. But it will be a transition for all of us. No matter what happens, we're proud of you, son." His phone buzzed, and he glanced at the screen.

"Who's that?" I asked, already knowing the answer. His boss was getting famous for reaching out at all hours.

Dad stuffed the phone in his pocket. "It's nothing." He kissed the top of my head. "It's been a long day. Get some sleep. Love you."

"Love you too." As he turned for the doorway, I felt like I needed to say something else. "Dad?"

"Yeah?"

"I'm sorry."

He scrunched his eyebrows. "About what?"

I sighed. "I don't know. All this college stuff being so expensive, I guess. I hate to put extra pressure on you with your new job. I can see if they'll give me some extra hours at FarmWorks."

He walked back and draped his arm over my shoulders. "Son, that is not anything you need to worry about. You're already working plenty. You just do your best in your studies, and your running, and get into the school that's right for you. Let us worry about the rest of it, okay?"

"Yeah, but it's not that easy, Dad." I stepped back so I could see his eyes. "I mean, there's no escaping it. Tech is expensive."

"That's true," Dad replied. "It is expensive. But I like to think of it more as an investment than a cost."

"Investment? Like a stock?"

He chuckled. "Sure, like a stock. But it's an investment in you. And there's no doubt in my mind that you're a growth company poised for amazing things. When opportunity knocks, you need to answer the door." He squeezed me again and said goodnight.

I stood in the dim kitchen and considered his words. Was he right? I'd always done well in my classes, but that was high school. College would be harder, and its consequences deeper and longer lasting. Did I have what it took to make it in the real world?

I got ready for bed, but I was still too wired to sleep. I was filled with sudden inspiration to start taking hold of my opportunities, so I began a letter to the computer science department on my laptop.

> *Thank you for taking the time to meet with me today. I was excited about the interesting scenarios that we talked through in the lab…*

I leaned back in my chair. That sounded stupid. Sleepiness crept into my brain. I reached to close the program, but an email alert flashed on the screen. The sender name read simply, *Visitor Services*, about as plain vanilla as it could get.

"Follow-up Invitation," the subject line read. "Time-sensitive information. Open immediately."

It all sounded suspicious. It could be spam, asking me to send money to someone in an isolated African kingdom or something else crazy. But then again, it could be connected to the Tech visit.

When I clicked on the email, the webcam light above my screen illuminated. A message box appeared. "Retinal identification commencing. Hold still."

Retinal identification? Since when did my laptop have technology like that? I figured it must be a virus, but before I could close the program, the light disappeared and the message box gave way to a stream of fast-moving green code.

The movement slowed until static words filled the center of the screen. It was a formal letter.

To: Bryce Pearson
Subject: Confidential

Congratulations. You have been selected to be one of a narrow group of prospective computer science students invited for a confidential assessment. This exclusive initiative was established to pull the very best programming minds from across the country. If selected, qualifying applicants will be eligible for full scholarships to the undergraduate and graduate institutions of their choosing.

That had to be a scam, but I kept reading.

Please arrive for your personal assessment at 5:00 PM, Friday, July 8th.

I did a quick search of the address listed at the bottom of the letter. It was several miles past Tech. It must be on the other side of the mountain.

Plan on spending two nights at our facilities. All lodging and meals will be taken care of. Pack clothes and toiletries, but everything else will be provided.

It is with the utmost seriousness that we ask you to keep this information completely confidential. Under no circumstances are you to share knowledge of this invitation with friends or even family members. While we realize this may seem unusual, you have been pre-screened with an elevated security clearance. More information will be provided upon successful completion of the interview and assessment.

This is a select honor, and we're extremely interested to meet with you. Exciting things lie ahead. To accept this invitation, click the icon below. This information will disappear in sixty seconds.

Sixty seconds? What the heck was this? Why was it so cloak-and-dagger? Who did they think I was, Jason Bourne?

I glanced at the clock in the corner of the screen. 11:30 PM. Maybe I was getting too tired.

I read the line about the scholarship again—a full ride through grad school. How was that even possible? I remembered my conversation with Dad. Could this be an opportunity knocking?

An alert flashed across the bottom of the screen.

This message will disappear in thirty seconds.

My heart beat fast. I tried to imagine who could have sent the message. I wiped my suddenly sweaty palms on my T-shirt.

A clock started flashing on the screen.

Ten seconds.

I had to make a decision.

Five seconds.

I clicked *Accept.*

I wasn't sure if I even meant to. In my mind I'd decided against it, but I clicked the button anyway. A jolt of energy shocked my fingers from the trackpad on the keyboard. I jerked my hand back, knocking a glass of water onto my lap and then the floor.

The location and time of my appointment flashed back on the screen with a reminder to copy down the information and to keep it secured. I ignored the spill, feverishly copying the address, date, and time.

I decided that the message was most likely from Dr. Hendrickson. It had to be. It wasn't from the track coach, that was for sure. But how could I get away for a whole weekend without telling Mom and Dad, or even Maggie, where I was going?

This was crazy.

CHAPTER SIX_

The trees flew by as I navigated up the curvy mountain roads in my old Mustang. It was the same route we'd taken to Tech, but this felt different. I'd told Maggie and my parents I was camping for the weekend with my friend Tony. He'd agreed to cover for me even though I hadn't told him why. I didn't like lying, but the invitation had been clear. Tell no one.

I'd almost let my true intentions slip to Zach. He'd seen me pack my best khakis when I was getting ready. I think he sensed something was up, but I'd asked him a quick question about *Kingdom,* and he appeared to forget about my bag.

The GPS led me past Tech's main entrance and toward the other side of the mountain. Tech was growing by leaps and bounds every year, so maybe I was headed to part of a campus expansion. I'd heard that several emerging technology companies were popping up nearby, led by past graduates who still lived in the area. Maybe I was heading to the headquarters of one of those. Dad said it helped the local economy for intellectual capital to stay in the region rather than be drained to Silicon Valley and the West Coast or New York.

Several miles later, I pulled into a parking lot of a large building. I took a deep breath. It felt like college was already beginning. Whatever was waiting for me inside that building was important. It could be my chance to prove myself to Professor Hendrickson and, if the message was true, cover my college tuition.

I took a moment before I got out of the car to pretend I was at a track meet, waiting for the starting gun to sound. It always focused my mind.

Runners, take your marks.

Get set.

Bang.

ENTERING THE BUILDING, I stepped into what felt like a doctor's office waiting room. In front of me were several rows of chairs and a reception counter with a sliding glass window. I counted four people sitting in the chairs, three guys and a girl, all about my age. They each stared at an identical electronic tablet. Most glanced up at me when I entered with my duffle bag but quickly returned to their devices.

I stepped up to the counter. A woman on the other side of the window typed at a laptop, but she didn't look my way. After a few seconds, I tapped on the glass. "Hello?"

She glanced up, surprised, as if it was highly unusual for someone to be at the window. She slid the glass to the side. "Can I help you?"

I tried to look confident. "Hi. I'm here for an interview?" Somehow my statement came out as a question.

"Look right there," the woman said with annoyance.

"Where?" I followed her glance toward the ceiling before a flash of light blinded me.

"There," she answered, after the mounted camera had already flashed. "Do you have a phone?"

I blinked, trying to see through the dark spots. "What?"

"If you have a cell phone, you'll need to relinquish it for the duration of your stay. It will be securely held until your departure."

I didn't like the sound of that, but wasn't sure I could refuse. I dug my phone from my pocket and begrudgingly handed it to her. "What if I need to contact someone?"

"We'll be able to assist with any communications in the event of an emergency." She sighed and handed me the same type of tablet the others in the room had. "Take a seat and read through the documents. Sign where it's marked." She closed the glass and went back to her typing.

I stood there for a moment, processing what had happened, before sitting in a row near the front. I clicked on the tablet. The documents were marked confidential and littered with serious language about non-disclosures. Each page required an electronic signature. I kept scrolling, but the pages went on forever.

"She's a bear, I'll warn you," a voice whispered behind me.

I turned to look at the guy seated in the next row, two chairs to my left. His red hair hung over his ears, and he projected the vibe of a skater who had tried to dress up but failed miserably.

"What?" I replied.

"The documents, I mean," he said with a chuckle and nodded at the receptionist. "But her too."

"Right. Thanks." I heard him shifting chairs, and suddenly he was right behind me.

"Charles Kilroy, but my friends call me Charlie."

I realized he was extending his hand, so I twisted around and shook it. "Bryce."

"You here for the interview?"

"Yeah." I wasn't sure if I should talk to him. We were both in the waiting room, but perhaps the top-secret instructions still applied.

He didn't seem too concerned. "You live nearby?"

I nodded. "Milton. You?"

"Edgarton."

That was a small town down this side of the mountain and at least a couple hours from Milton. I tried to focus back on the documents, but they were written in a style that you'd have to be a lawyer to understand.

Charlie seemed to sense my thoughts and laughed. "I don't know what the hell they say either. I just signed it all. I mean, we've come this far, right? I need some excitement in my summer vacation."

I frowned, trying to think of a response, but was saved from answering when the door from outside opened and a girl entered. I automatically sized her up like the rest of them, as if we were all competing for a big job. And who knows, maybe we were. The new girl was short and slender. She wore fashionable, dark-rimmed glasses, with her straight black hair pulled back and pinned to the top of her head. Unlike Charlie, she was dressed formally. Her navy suit jacket and skirt made it look like she was interviewing for a corporate accounting position. She was pretty, but she seemed to be working hard to hide it.

I decided to drop my guard a level. "Any idea what we're doing here?" I asked Charlie.

"Maybe one or two." He glanced around the room and then back at me. "Let me guess, you're an ace with computers?"

I nodded. It made sense that we'd be similar. And the invitation had said I'd been selected from a pool of computer science students.

"Top of your class?"

I nodded again.

"Me too."

Both Charlie and I looked over as the dark-haired girl sat in my row, two seats away. I think she could sense we were staring at her, and she glanced up and smiled politely.

Charlie leaned toward her. "So, what's your situation?"

"Excuse me?" she replied coldly.

I noticed a mark poking out from beneath her shirtsleeve that didn't fit with the rest of her look—a small crescent moon tattoo on her wrist.

Charlie tried again. "Sorry, I meant, are you a programmer?"

She lowered her tablet and eyed us carefully. "It says we're not supposed to be talking to anyone. Didn't you read this?"

"Do you understand it?" I asked.

She bit her lip. "Some of it. But they make it painfully clear that we're not supposed to discuss anything."

Charlie waved his hand. "What are they gonna do, lock us in?"

I smiled and tried to act friendly. "I'm Bryce."

She sighed, but her expression softened. "Rachel. Nice to meet you."

"I'm Charlie."

Her frown returned. "Charming."

"So, you don't know what this is about either?" I asked.

Rachel shook her head. "No, I just received an electronic message after visiting Wickman."

"Wickman College?" asked Charlie.

Rachel nodded. Wickman was near the border of the next state over. I knew it had a strong computer science program and it was on my list of potential schools to visit.

She looked at me. "How about you?"

"I'm hoping to go to Tech." I turned to Charlie. "You too?"

He shook his head. "No, I'm going out west. USC or Stanford if I can get in." He glanced toward the door. "Need to spread my wings."

I considered what they'd both said. All three of us seemed to have arrived without any hard facts. "I wonder what it means that we're all from different places and looking at different schools."

Rachel shrugged. "Probably nothing."

"Makes it easier to keep things quiet," said Charlie. "Who knows what these birdwatchers are up to?"

I don't know if she saw us talking, but the receptionist slid the window back and called for everyone's tablets. I hadn't finished reading, but I followed Charlie's lead and just signed my name at all the highlighted spots. I returned the tablet as a door opened next to the counter. A man wearing a suit stepped into the waiting room.

"Good evening, everyone," he said. "Please follow me."

And that's how it began.

CHAPTER SEVEN_

I remember reading *Alice in Wonderland* when I was a kid. And watching the first *Matrix* movie—the good one. The blue pill or the red pill, the rabbit hole, they both share a common theme. They are ways of delving into an existence that you never even knew was possible. That's what stepping through that doorway with Rachel and Charlie became. None of us knew what lay inside, and after we entered, everything changed.

"Please take a seat by the card with your name."

We'd followed the man down a winding corridor, ending up in this standard-looking classroom. There were four long tables with three chairs at each, an instructor's desk in the front, and a large monitor on the wall. The video board looked crazy high-tech, but otherwise it could have been a classroom at Milton High. There were six of us altogether, but I was pleased to be seated in the front row with Charlie and Rachel. The other three sat in the row behind us.

The man cleared his throat. "I'm Dr. Johannes Sturgis. Welcome to orientation." He glanced at his tablet and then back at us. "You may have noticed you're seated in two distinct groups. The people at your table will be your working team for the weekend. For simplicity's sake, we'll call this first table the Red Team." He glanced at our table and ticked off our names. "Rachel Kelly, Bryce Pearson, and Charles Kilroy."

"It's Charlie."

Dr. Sturgis nodded, but didn't change his introduction. He looked past us to the second table. "And the Blue Team." He consulted his notes once more. "Amanda Sefing, Connor Newell, and Tito Morales."

I turned and eyed the others. So we weren't just in this for ourselves. We were competing against the other team. Competing for what, I wasn't certain, but I was glad that I'd met Charlie and Rachel in the waiting room.

Sturgis leaned against the front desk and stared back at us seriously. "You've already been told, but I need to remind you that everything you see or hear during this orientation is highly confidential. You are not to tell anyone outside this room of the projects that you will work on. One of the documents you signed earlier is a full nondisclosure statement, which, I assure you, we enforce to the utmost. You've each been carefully selected for this opportunity. I implore you not to take it lightly."

A hand raised behind me. Sturgis begrudgingly paused and acknowledged it. "Yes?"

"What opportunity?" Connor asked. "What project are we even here for?"

Apparently no one knew why they were here.

Sturgis nodded. "I promise, answers will be provided in good time." He left it at that and stood and walked around the desk.

"But apparently not right now," Charlie whispered.

Sturgis returned and handed us each a silver laptop. "These are your workstations for the weekend. Please go ahead and activate your laptop using the fingerprint sensor in the trackpad and the retinal scanner in the webcam. These are your only login credentials and will ensure the maximum security. Guard this device with your life."

I raised my eyebrows at his dramatic remark.

"For those of you who progress past the orientation program, these will be yours to take home and will be our communication link throughout the program. While they are fully secure, I urge you to treat these computers with the utmost care."

We opened the laptops and followed some initial login instructions. I placed my thumb on the trackpad and a scan of my print appeared on the screen. I then bent down and stared into the camera above the screen. A red light flashed at me and a message popped up.

User identification instituted. Bryce Pearson confirmed.

It was cool but a little freaky.

Once we'd all logged in, Dr. Sturgis continued his speech. "I'm introducing you to the orientation program, but you'll primarily work with our team of instructors. In a moment, you will bring your luggage and laptops into your private sleeping rooms. You'll then have a quick meal in our cafeteria before starting a series of individual assessments."

"What kind of assessments?" asked Rachel.

Sturgis attempted a smile, but it came off more like a leer. "Each of you will have rigorous skills, aptitude, and IQ tests, and a polygraph evaluation this evening. Tomorrow is a group programming activity, and for those who advance, Sunday will be a comprehensive tour of our state-of-the-art computer lab and programming facilities."

I didn't know whether I should be excited or petrified.

"Come on now, Doc, be straight with us. Am I here because of my kick-ass scores in *Final Kingdom*?" Charlie asked.

Sturgis paused, a brief hint of transparency filling his face, but then he carried on as usual. "You're closer to the truth than you'd think, Mr. Kilroy. But for now, just know that each of you is here for a reason. You're the best programming minds from any of the high schools in this region."

I thought about the classes I'd finished junior year. This place didn't feel like high school. It was different.

"What about the full scholarship stuff in the message?" said Tito, glancing around like he'd spilled a secret. "Or was I the only one that got that?"

"Cost-free acceptance into the university and graduate school of your choosing is one of the benefits offered to anyone successfully entering our program," Sturgis explained.

Charlie whistled.

"And you'll put that in writing?" asked Amanda.

"We'll arrange everything," Sturgis said cryptically. "As I've said, our work here is highly confidential. We're breaking barriers like mankind has never seen before. It's an exciting time to be a part of our mission."

We looked at each other, trying to decide if he was serious or just putting us on.

A knock sounded at the door and Sturgis waved his hand. "And that's our signal to move along. We have a tight schedule. I'll see you after your meal."

We were escorted to an elevator that took us to the fourth

floor. Everything on this level looked like a hotel. The doors were all marked with alternating room numbers on both sides, and a carpet ran down the center of the hallway. We were each given a separate room assignment, told to unpack and be ready for dinner downstairs in fifteen minutes.

My rectangular room was small, but clean. The ceilings were higher than I was used to, and the only external light came from two narrow horizontal windows on the far wall. They were high enough that even perched on the edge of the steel bedframe, I couldn't see out of them.

I placed my clothes in a small dresser, my toiletries in the bathroom, and then sat on the edge of the bed, wondering how I had arrived at this place. Should I have told my parents where I was headed? If anything went wrong, no one in the world would know where to find me. Mom, Dad, Zach, or even Maggie wouldn't know where to start looking.

A knock at the door pushed those thoughts from my mind. I got up and saw Charlie's distorted face through the peephole in the door. It hadn't had been fifteen minutes, but I let him in.

"Hey," said Charlie, but instead of following me into the room, he turned into the bathroom, waving for me to follow.

I raised my eyebrows but did as he asked. "What's wrong?"

Charlie put his finger to his lips and whispered. "Did you see the camera?"

"Camera?" I hadn't noticed anything, but then again, I hadn't been looking. "There's a camera in your room?"

"Shh!" Charlie leaned on the corner of the doorframe, and casually pointed to a sprinkler system head in the ceiling. "They're watching us."

I glanced at the ceiling. "Who?"

Charlie frowned. "Santa Claus. Jeez, Bryce. Who do you think?"

"You mean Sturgis?" I said, trying to follow along. "Why would he be watching us?"

"Maybe for the same reason they took our phones. This whole thing has an odd bent."

"Is that even legal?"

Charlie shrugged. "Who knows? I think these guys get off on acting like they're above the law."

"I think you're paranoid."

"We'll see soon enough." He turned to the hallway door. "Come on, let's get Rachel and head down to dinner."

CHAPTER EIGHT_

The food was good, but conversation was light as we sat around the table at dinner. Charlie and Rachel seemed to have the same whirlwind of questions spinning through their heads as I did. We were all wondering what lay around the next corner of the maze.

After the meal, we were led to separate rooms. Mine was cramped and windowless, with only a small table and chair, like an interrogation room at a police station. Another sprinkler-type object hung down from the ceiling. I wondered if they really were watching us, or if Charlie's paranoia was just wearing off on me. Of course, it could all just be an innocent security precaution, but it gave me the willies.

On the table was a tablet that already had a question waiting for my answer as I sat down. I'd never taken an IQ test before, but it seemed like that's what this was. It was impossible to know how you were doing. Most of the answers weren't fully right or fully wrong, more like shades of gray. I also couldn't tell how far from the end I was, as the next question just kept coming up on the tablet. The next test was several dozen complex questions about programming. There were two I wasn't sure about, but overall I thought I did okay. The screen instructed me to report to Examination Room C as the door buzzed and cracked open. I hadn't even realized they'd locked me in.

I assumed I was headed to another assessment, but the phrase "examination room" heightened my sense of being a subject in someone's science project. I found the room and sat in the only chair, which was outfitted with an enhanced armrest, like in the doctor's office where they drew blood samples before track season. A computer and monitor were next to my chair, with an assortment of odd wires extending to the floor. It was either a sophisticated torture device or the polygraph machine Sturgis had mentioned.

I waited in the chair for what seemed like a long time. I was about to stand up and check that I'd entered the correct exam room, when the door opened. I swallowed hard as a strikingly beautiful woman in a white lab coat walked in. She appeared to be in her twenties, with blonde hair artfully pulled back in a clip.

"Good evening, Bryce," she said in a heavily accented voice. I tried to place whether it was British or Australian. I felt my heart racing as she shook my hand a bit longer than needed. Her skin was soft, but I forced my mind to focus on what she was saying. "My name is Dr. Avanair. But please, call me Heather."

"Hi," I answered, trying not to squirm in my seat.

"Have you taken a polygraph before?"

She was Australian. I was sure of it. In my excitement at figuring it out, I nearly forgot her question. I shook my head. "No."

Heather nodded as she straightened the assortment of wires and switched on the monitor. "We use this as part of our security clearance. It collects a series of physiological responses from different systems in the body. Stand up, please."

I stood, and she placed a square pad on the seat of my chair that was connected to the computer.

"Now I'll need to strap these monitors around your chest." She leaned closer to me and wrapped a black tube below my arms and another around my stomach.

I caught a faint whiff of her perfume but tried to ignore it. As a distraction, I pictured Maggie back home. Fridays she usually worked late at the dress store, but would likely be heading home soon. Thinking of Maggie made me remember that she thought I was camping with Tony, but I tried to push back any feelings of guilt. If I got a full scholarship, we could go to Tech together and experience college the way we had planned. I was doing this for her too. I eyed the polygraph, wondering if it could read my every thought.

Heather wrapped a band like a blood pressure cuff around my arm and then attached clips to some of the fingers on my right hand. "I'm sorry if this is uncomfortable, but there's nothing to worry about. It won't hurt."

She moved to the other side of the monitor. "Just sit still and clear your mind."

I took a deep breath. Easier said than done.

"I will ask you a series of baseline questions first." She spoke calmly as she typed on the computer. She glanced up and smiled, expertly batting her eyelashes like she knew very well the effect she had on men. "Please answer with only a simple 'yes' or 'no.' Okay?"

"Got it. I mean, yes." I wondered if she was the one who

administered this test to all the recruits, or just to the high school boys. If this was a scheme to distract and get blood pressure racing, it was working.

"Excellent. Let's begin." She pressed a button, and I felt the sleeve tighten on my arm. I tried to stay calm, not to tense up, but it was nearly impossible under the circumstances.

"Is your name Bryce Pearson?"

"Yes."

"Do you live at 56 Morehead Road?"

"Yes." So far so good. Maybe this would be easier than I'd feared.

"Are you seventeen years old?"

"Yes."

There were several more straightforward, factual questions that were easy to answer. I started to get comfortable.

"Have you ever gone skydiving?"

I raised my eyebrows a little. That was different. "No."

"Do you love your parents?"

"Yes."

"Have you ever lied to them?"

I hesitated, glancing at the back of the monitor, wondering what signals my body was giving. "Yes."

"Did you tell them the true nature of your visit this weekend?"

"No."

"Have you told anyone about coming here?"

"No."

"Are you dating Maggie Palmer?"

"Yes." How would they know about Maggie? What did she have to do with this? They must have run an extensive background check.

"Are you in love with her?"

"Um, I think so." The room was air conditioned, but I was getting warm. I felt sweat forming on my forehead.

Heather glanced at me. "Please keep your answers to yes or no. Are you in love with her?"

"Yes."

"Have you ever cheated on a test in high school?"

My mind rewound. There was that time when Tyson helped me with the lab experiment in Biology, but was that cheating?

"Bryce?"

I guess I thought about it too long.

"Sorry. No."

"Are you currently, or have you ever been, in the employment of the United States Government?"

I tried to answer faster. Maybe it was better just to answer without thinking. "No."

"Have you ever worked for, or been under the control of, a foreign national power?"

Foreign power? What the heck? "No."

"Are you telling the truth on all of your answers?"

"Yes."

"Are you known under the ID *BeeRice4u* on the video game *Final Kingdom*?"

I chuckled, realizing how dumb it sounded. "Yes." How did they know my ID in *Kingdom*?

The test went on for another ten minutes, following the same style of questioning. When it was over, Heather walked back to my chair and unhooked the monitors.

"That's it?" I asked, exhaling.

"Would you like more?"

"Uh, no, I'm good."

"Then we're finished. I told you it was easy." She rested her hand on my shoulder as she unhooked the chest strap. "You did great, Bryce."

"Thanks." I looked up and saw she was smiling at me. "So, what's next? Walking over hot coals?"

She opened the door to the hall. "No, that's not until tomorrow."

I raised my eyebrows.

Heather chuckled. "You can head back to your room for the night. Get some rest. You're in for a real treat. In the morning, you're scheduled for the group programming competition."

When the door to my room locked behind me, I tried to remind myself I wasn't in a prison cell. I glanced up at the sprinkler. There were so many things that didn't make sense at this place.

Too many.

With no phone to check or way of amusing myself, I got into bed, trying to fall asleep, and trying not to think about Heather Avanair and her sexy Australian accent.

CHAPTER NINE_

I sat up quickly in bed. What was that sound? In the darkness, it took me a moment to remember where I was sleeping. The clock on the table read 3:30. Every ten seconds a red light flashed from the sprinkler in the ceiling.

I stumbled to my feet and moved lightly across the unfamiliar room. I made it to the bathroom, flipping the lights on momentarily to get my bearings, but turning them off quickly so as not to be blinded. I took a drink of water from the tap with my hand and then used the toilet.

That's when I heard the voice.

The sound had come from the ceiling. Were there cameras that had some kind of speakers in the bathroom too, or was I still asleep and this was all a dream?

Then it came again. Quiet, but pleading. "Hello? Can you hear me?"

I isolated the voice to an air vent near the ceiling. "Who's there?" I whispered back.

"You can't let them take me!"

The voice was male, but I didn't recognize it. As far as I

knew, only the recruits from the Red and Blue Teams were sleeping in these rooms, but the compound was huge, and I had the sneaking suspicion that I'd only scratched the surface of things.

"Take you where?" I asked.

"There's no time." His voice sounded desperate. "You don't know what you're involved in. I'm warning you. There's so much more."

A door shut further down the hallway. I moved back to the room and peered through the peephole in the door, but the hall was dark except for a glow from an emergency floodlight. It was green and eerie. I rubbed my eyes and went back into the bathroom.

"It's them," the voice cried. "They're coming for me."

I heard several sets of footsteps in the hall, like a group was walking toward my room.

"You have to find Tyler," said the voice, clearer now, like he was pressed up against the vent in his room. "Send him the code. He can use it in their machine. Project JOSHUA. Promise me!"

My mind was spinning. What was he talking about?

"Who are you?" I whispered.

The footsteps in the hall stopped. The lock clicked open in the room next to mine.

"It's too late," the voice hissed. "They're here. Promise me you'll find Tyler!"

"Okay," I answered. "I promise."

There was a crash, like he had fallen back down to the floor as they forced his door open. I heard the sound of people bursting in, screams as they dragged him into the hall, his hands banging on the walls, desperately clutching at anything that might save him.

His cries grew farther and farther away, until finally a door slammed, echoing through the now-deserted hallway. Then everything was silent.

I stood motionless behind my door, my heart galloping in my chest. When the hallway remained quiet, I eventually got back in my bed, but I was wide awake and replaying the memory of what I'd heard. Was he a recruit like the rest of us? What code was he talking about? And who was Tyler?

* * *

I WOKE TO A REPETITIVE RINGING. It was disorienting at first, but soon I scrambled to my feet and turned off the alarm clock I hadn't set. I looked through the peephole, but the hall was empty. I'd showered and dressed by the time my door lock released. Before turning down the hallway toward breakfast, I noticed the door to the next room was open. The room looked exactly like mine, but it was vacant. The bed was perfectly made, and there were no bags or other signs of anyone staying there. Maybe it was all a dream.

I found my way downstairs to the cafeteria, where Charlie and Rachel were already eating.

"Morning." Charlie pointed to a buffet line. "Food's over there. Pretty good, too, believe it or not."

I filled a plate with eggs, hash browns, and toast and walked back to the table. Dr. Sturgis was at a nearby table, speaking to the Blue Team.

"How'd you sleep?" asked Charlie.

"Not very well," I said.

"You heard it too?" Rachel's eyes darted to Sturgis, then back to me. "I thought I dreamt it until I spoke to Charlie."

"It was the room right next to mine."

Charlie raised his eyebrows. "Who was it?"

"I don't know." I considered whether I should tell them about the warning the voice gave me and the message for Tyler, but Dr. Sturgis stepped up to our table before I could make up my mind.

He smiled and patted Charlie on the back. "Good morning, candidates. I trust you all slept well?"

Was he serious? Did he not know about the screaming in the middle of the night? Or was he just messing with us? Maybe this was just another test.

"Not exactly," answered Charlie.

"I do apologize for any disruptions during the night. I was just explaining the same issue to the Blue Team." Sturgis nodded like he was relaying the weather.

"What happened?" asked Rachel.

"I'm afraid that a former recruit had to be removed from the program," Sturgis went on, his expression more like he'd extracted a tooth instead of a person. "We can only have the very best."

"Removed?" I asked. "In the middle of the night?"

Sturgis nodded. "It doesn't happen often, but the individual could not adhere to our *terms*." He said it offhandedly, as if the guy had been found too young to play the lottery.

"What happened to him?" Rachel repeated.

"He was escorted off the premises," Sturgis answered, and then swiftly changed the subject. "But we have a busy day planned for you today. Your group instructor will be here shortly to start your programming test." He glanced over our heads. "Ah, here she is now."

I turned to see a familiar face.

"Team, I'd like you to meet Dr. Avanair. She's our programming coordinator and head psychological evaluator. You will be working with her extensively if you make it through the weekend."

I didn't like the way he said that, as if being dragged out in the middle of the night was a possibility for us all.

"Good morning, everyone," Heather said in her Australian accent. I felt my stomach do a somersault.

"Damn," Charlie muttered.

From Charlie's reaction, it seemed this was the first he was seeing of Heather.

"I'll be administering your programming skills test this morning," Heather explained. "You'll be working together as a team to develop unique solutions for our progressive streaming code. The team who best meets the objectives of the project will advance."

"What happens to the losing team?" I asked. Would they be "escorted off the premises" as well? Sounds of screaming still echoed in my memory.

Heather's face showed no emotion. "They will not advance."

I tried to gear myself up for the challenge. I'd never been one to turn away from a competition, and with a college scholarship dangling at the end of this rope, I needed to do everything possible to make that opportunity happen, for me and for my family.

Heather instructed us to meet her in the seminar room in ten minutes. Charlie gave me a look as she left the room.

"I know," I said. "I met her yesterday."

Rachel rolled her eyes. "Keep it in your pants, you two."

"Sorry," Charlie replied. "I've got a thing for chicks with accents. It's hot."

Rachel waved her hand. "Forget it. I've got three brothers. I know the drill. But we have to focus if we're going to win this. We have to be able to rely on each other." She looked at us seriously. "I need this scholarship. Can I count on you two?"

"Absolutely," I said, matching her determined stare. "I need it too."

Charlie chuckled. "Let's light this candle."

Rachel stared at him again. "I'm serious, Charlie."

He sighed. "What? I *am* serious. I probably need the money more than both of you two combined. You can count on me."

I downed the rest of my orange juice. "Do you buy his explanation of the noises last night?"

Charlie shook his head. "I don't trust those fibberlickers." He grinned like he'd just made that one up on the spot.

"I'm not sure," said Rachel, "but what choice do we have? For now we just have to do what they tell us."

"This whole thing went left a while ago," said Charlie. "We're locked up in this lab like rats in a maze. We might as well try to make it to the cheese."

We piled up our trash and walked to the door. I wondered if there was more than just a slice of cheese waiting for us.

CHAPTER TEN_

"Which of you had the question yesterday about *Final Kingdom*?" Heather asked the group. Red and Blue Teams were sitting at tables again, this time facing head-on so we wouldn't see each other's screens.

"That was me," said Charlie. "It rocks."

Heather smiled. "Well, Mr. Kilroy, you'll be happy to learn that *Final Kingdom* is the paradigm world for which you will be developing code in our group competition today. Each group will be tasked with constructing an interface that will uniquely connect to the game."

Connor's hand went up from the other table.

"Yes?" said Heather.

"What if someone doesn't play *Kingdom*? That doesn't seem fair."

Heather sighed. "Let's take a quick poll. How many of you play *Kingdom*?

All six hands across the two teams rose quickly.

"And how many of you would say you're not just good,

but the very best *Kingdom* player of anyone you know at your school or in your social group?"

Again, all six hands went up. Low murmurs began filling the room. What was going on?

Heather switched on the wall monitor. *Kingdom's* welcome screen flashed before us. "As you may have started to realize, despite *Kingdom's* widespread popularity, this is not just a simple coincidence. Q2, the developer of *Final Kingdom*, is a division of our operation here."

We all stared, dumbfounded at the possibility that this could be true.

"What you don't likely realize is that we have been utilizing *Kingdom* for over a year now as a primary selection tool for this recruitment program."

My mouth dropped open.

"Get out of town," scoffed Charlie.

Heather nodded patiently, like she'd heard such skepticism before. "We've designed it with complex problem solving and logistical thinking built right into the game, so that it is now an incredibly accurate marker for determining success here in our program."

"Wait a minute," said Amanda from the Blue Team. "So you just pick out good video game players? What if they're, like, ten years old?"

"Well of course, that's only one marker we look for," Heather replied. "We look at a wide range of information—academic performance, age, and competitive ability. It's also not a coincidence that you are all about to begin your senior year of high school. The program requires a degree of maturity that is normally only achieved by students your age."

"So we're just here to build video games?" said Tito.

"That's all well and good, but my ambitions go higher than that."

Heather leaned against the front of her desk. "Fear not. I assure you we're doing much more than that. But all will be revealed in good time." She brought up a list of instructions to the screen. "Let's get started. You have the entire day to work together. You may access the conference rooms next door for private brainstorming, but you must end at 8:00 PM, regardless of the status of your work. Presentations will be made later this evening. The winning team will advance and complete your initiation tomorrow with an extensive tour of our programming facilities."

"And the losing team?" asked Rachel.

"One team will not make it. And I'm sorry, but we don't offer parting gifts. Our association will end, and you will not qualify for any of the scholarship opportunities. Again, I will remind you that even if you are unsuccessful, you are still legally bound under the terms of all the confidentiality agreements that you signed upon your arrival." She stood and walked to the door. "Good luck."

Building something unique to interface with *Kingdom* was a broad category, but it got our creative juices flowing. We brainstormed in the conference room for the first two hours, landing on a concept and development map, and then we each went to work on individual tasks. Charlie was in charge of the design elements, Rachel the backend interface within the game code, and I was dealing with the delivery language, which would make our solution able to appear where it needed to within the game. We didn't know what the Blue Team was working on, but with less than twelve hours to execute our idea, we couldn't afford to worry about them.

At around two o'clock, we realized we hadn't had lunch, so we took a thirty-minute break to hit the cafeteria together. Sometimes recharging the body was the best sort of exercise for the mind.

"I still can't get over what she said about *Kingdom*," Rachel muttered between bites of her pasta salad.

"All this time, they've been watching us?" I asked. "Tracking our moves within the game? Is that legal?"

"I told you," said Charlie. "They're above the law. My old man used to say that some people just think they're better than everyone else and that they don't have to follow the rules."

"I don't know if that's true," said Rachel.

Charlie took a large bite of his sandwich. "Yeah, it's probably why he hasn't come home in five years."

I raised my eyebrows. "Your dad hasn't come home in five years? Why not?"

"I'm sure he'd like to," Charlie said, "but he's got ten more years to go on his sentence."

"Oh," was all I could say, suddenly feeling bad. I hadn't realized his dad was in prison.

"I'm so sorry," said Rachel.

Charlie shrugged. "What are you gonna do, right? He thought he could get away with it." He nodded back at Rachel. "How 'bout you? What's your family like? Let me guess…doctors? Or maybe lawyers. Or one of each?"

Rachel frowned. "Stop. It's not like that. My mom's a dental hygienist. But my folks split up a year ago. Dad lives in Florida. He's a tax accountant." She turned to me. "Are your parents together, Bryce?"

"Yeah. Mom works at a PR firm and Dad's in sales, but he got laid off a few months back and money's tight now with his new job. They're always stressing about how to pay for school next year. That's one of the reasons I jumped at this chance."

"So I guess we'd better win," said Charlie. "Or we're all screwed."

We laughed as we finished our food. "Have you ever been to the house of mirrors at the amusement park?" Rachel asked.

I nodded. "Sure, everything's all distorted, and you can't tell which image is the real one."

"Kind of like my dad after one of his benders," said Charlie.

Rachel grimaced, but kept talking. "I have an idea."

"For our code?" I asked.

She nodded. "I think this could put us over the top. Come on, let's get back to work."

* * *

WE NEVER GOT to hear the Blue Team's project. Each group presented their ideas separately to Heather and Dr. Sturgis. Ours had changed a couple times during development, but what we landed on was pretty awesome. I'd never been one of those runners who pukes before the start of a big race, but as we stepped into the room that night for our presentation, my stomach was churning.

"Whenever you're ready," said Heather, sitting with Sturgis in the middle of the room as Charlie, Rachel and I stood up front. A video conferencing unit was positioned next to them as if someone was watching remotely, but they didn't say who it was. A local, offline *Kingdom* test site was loaded onto our computer and displayed on the monitor behind us.

Charlie started the presentation. "Imagine that you're

playing *Kingdom* in the middle of an intense round." He grinned at Heather and Sturgis. "You know, really kicking ass."

"We get the point, Mr. Kilroy," said Sturgis. "Please continue."

"But there's a Ranger on your tail, and you need a diversion," said Rachel, chiming in before Charlie got too far off the rails. "What if you could institute a hologram, a duplicate of yourself, or another image that could temporarily confuse your enemy, providing time for a last-minute escape?"

I stepped forward and activated the game sequence with a controller in my hand. "Our new code creates the ability to project yourself anywhere within the game with the push of a button." I demonstrated how a player's avatar could be running in a field, and then when an attacker tried to shoot them, it was revealed that the avatar was only a hologram. The true player was safely hiding in the trees. "Like being in a house of mirrors," I added, smiling at Rachel.

"Interesting," said Sturgis. "I like the way you activated that with the controller as well."

"Thank you," said Rachel. "Any questions?"

"Can the hologram communicate?" asked Heather. "Is it auditory too, or only visual?"

"Right now, it's just the visual hologram," Rachel explained. "Perhaps that could be developed down the road. But what we did build was the ability to design the hologram to be whatever image you'd like—a copy of your own player's avatar, an object, an animal, or even another avatar in the game."

"But here's the best part," said Charlie, nodding to me. "Bryce really killed it here. It's genius."

I smiled and switched screens to show the programming

map and code. "We designed the delivery mechanism so it uses the electrical impulses from within the game to transmit the image. This creates a portability that opens the doors to uses in the real world, and not just within *Kingdom*."

"Like what?" asked Sturgis.

I tried to remain confident. It was just a theory I'd had, but I was pretty sure it could work. "Because we're using existing electrical impulses, there's no end to the applications where it could fit. Instead of the game, you could use cellular networks, for example."

Sturgis leaned toward the video conferencing device, then nodded and whispered something in Heather's ear. They both began to clap. "Astounding, Bryce," Sturgis said.

"All three of you, very good work," added Heather.

We grinned and high-fived each other at the front of the room. The Blue Team seemed sharp, but I knew our idea would be tough to beat.

CHAPTER ELEVEN_

We won in a landslide.

The next morning at the results reveal, Heather said it wasn't even close. They loved our design application and the potential to expand beyond the game. Sturgis even said he could imagine applying for a patent for my delivery mechanism.

The Blue Team didn't take it well. Connor argued with Heather that the competition had been rigged. It was hard to watch their dejected faces as they filed out of the room. I trusted that Sturgis was telling the truth and that they were being sent home, but didn't think about it for long. We quickly turned toward each other and celebrated.

"Congratulations," said Heather, walking over and shaking my hand.

"You don't look very surprised that we won," I said.

She smiled knowingly. "Are you?"

I shrugged. "A little. It's all a lot to take in."

"I never doubted you."

Charlie cleared his throat. "You mean us, right? It's not

like Bryce won on his own. Rachel and I helped too, you know."

Heather nodded, but gave me a quick wink. "Of course. It was a team effort."

"What happens now?" asked Rachel.

"Now…" Heather paused dramatically and opened the door, "we pull back the curtain."

She directed us down the hall to the elevator bank. Inside we waited for her to swipe her fingerprint on the scanner, but she pushed an unmarked button on the panel instead. A metal cover slid down from a section in the wall just above the floor numbers, and a green light scanned Heather's face. Then she stepped back with the rest of us as the elevator sank farther into the building, several levels beneath the ground. What was down here?

"Whoa," whistled Charlie, when the doors opened to a wide room that bustled with activity. "Welcome to La La Land."

We stepped forward to a metal railing and a platform overlooking a large room about the size of our school gym. But that was where the similarities ended. This place reminded me of operations central for NASA. A huge video board as big as a movie screen at a theater filled the far wall. It was divided into a dozen different views—images that appeared to be from security cameras, lines of streaming code, mathematical equations, and even satellite video filled the boxes. But instead of the satellite images being of recognizable locations like New York or Paris, they were from different levels within *Kingdom* —I saw Grant's Gorge, a jungle, a wide orange and red rocky desert plateau, a snowcapped peak in the mountains, a lazy country farm. But why?

Dozens of workstations were positioned around the room, each filled with men and women working at keyboards or standing over illuminated glass tables that seemed to function like giant horizontal tablets. Other people were buzzing about, coming and going like in a newsroom.

"What is this place?" I asked.

Heather smiled. "This is the heart of our operations, our central programming lab."

"And all these people?" asked Rachel, her mouth gaping in amazement just like mine.

"The best of the best," said Heather. "All former candidates like you, recruited from the top high schools and institutions from around the globe to create the most advanced programming team the world has ever known."

"Are they all working on the same thing?" asked Charlie.

"We have many different projects," answered Heather, "some just in their infancy, others more advanced. Think of it as an enormous technological incubator where the world's top minds develop innovations that will change our society forever."

I noticed that the left section of the room differed from the rest. A cluster of workstations was centered around a giant machine the size of a cement truck. I suspected it could be a supercomputer, but the image that kept coming to my mind was that of a spaceship.

Heather seemed to notice my gaze. "That is our most important project. The Eden Machine. It's what the three of you will be working on."

She glanced across the room to the wall opposite the machine. I noticed a bank of tall, curtained windows near the ceiling that reminded me of a luxury box at a sports arena. A curtain shook like someone had been standing there, watching us, but I didn't see anyone.

"What does it do?" asked Rachel, bringing my attention back to the Eden Machine.

"Why don't you go see for yourselves?" Heather directed us down a metal staircase and through the maze of computers until we were standing in front of the machine. It had a reflective silver shell, with an array of green lights scattered on all sides.

At a central workstation in the front of the machine was an enormously fat man. He leaned into a monitor, hammering at the keyboard in front of him and muttering an assortment of curse words. His desk was a mess, littered with soda cans and junk food wrappers.

Heather cleared her throat. "Mr. Fitz, may we have a moment of your time?"

The man glanced up as if he had been oblivious to anyone else in the room, despite the buzzing all around him.

"What? Oh, hello, Dr. Avanair..." He leered at her for a long moment. "So good to *see* you." He noticed us and attempted a smile, but his teeth were a mess and his face made me want to hurl. He didn't stand, but he wheeled his oversized chair toward us. It groaned under his weight as it slid across the floor. "And who have we here?"

"These are our newest recruits," Heather said coldly. "Bryce, Rachel, and Charles."

"It's Charlie."

Fitz extended his hand, and I reluctantly reached out and shook it. "Nice to meet you."

"Hi," said Rachel, shrinking back as if she also sensed a vile nature in the man.

"I was just explaining that the group will be joining your efforts here on Eden," said Heather.

Fitz nodded and shot us another nasty grin. "Wonderful."

When he didn't say more, Heather stepped closer. "I was hoping you might be able to give them an overview of your operation." She didn't seem to enjoy being near the man either.

Fitz grunted. "Oh, of course. I'd be happy to." He pointed at three chairs that were covered with piles of papers and trash. "Grab a seat."

We moved the junk to the floor and slid the chairs just close enough that we could see and hear what Fitz had to say.

"I'll be back to retrieve you three in a bit," said Heather. She glanced at Fitz uneasily, as if worried he might somehow infect her new recruits.

Fitz hammered again at his computer keyboard. Despite his large size, his meaty fingers seemed to fly over the keys with ease. An assortment of images flashed across his monitor. He pushed a final button, replicating his screen onto a corner of the enormous wall monitor.

"There, that will be easiest for you all to see." He turned toward us. "How much has Dr. Avanair explained to you?"

"Not much," replied Charlie.

Fitz sighed. "What a surprise. Well, lucky for you three, you've come to the right place. This entire facility was my idea. Or at least the part tied in to Eden."

I squinted at the screen, trying to make sense of what it projected. "What is Eden, exactly?"

"Good god," Fitz exclaimed. "I always forget how they keep you newbs in the dark." He glanced at the luxury box windows behind us, but then his expression turned sinister.

"Prepare to have your minds blown. Five years ago, we made a groundbreaking advancement in the science of physics." He glanced at us skeptically. "You have been educated in physics, correct? Or have they lowered the standards for recruits even further?"

We all nodded. "I received the highest grade in my AP class," said Rachel.

Fitz chuckled. "That's lovely, sweetheart. In a rudimentary sense, that may be comparable to what we're doing here, but only in the same way that a rowboat is similar to an aircraft carrier. They both move through the water, yet on fully different scales." He pressed a key and the images shifted on the screen. "The advanced physics we undertake here, a type of quantum computing, has the ability to transport humankind beyond the limits of our current physical dimension."

"Excuse me?" asked Charlie.

"Did you say another dimension?" asked Rachel.

Fitz's lips formed into another disgusting grin. "We are working on the ability to cross the digital divide to a new universe of possibility. Your children will view the work we're doing here the same way we look back at the Kennedy administration's race into space against the Soviets."

My head was spinning. I didn't remember learning any of this in physics class. "So this is like…a time travel device?"

Charlie snickered. "That's impossible."

Fitz shot him a glare. "We don't use that word here, Chuck. Artificial Intelligence has pushed the boundaries of what is possible beyond our imaginations."

"And that's why we're here?" asked Rachel. "To help build a transport system into another dimension? Are you serious?"

Fitz nodded. "I never joke about science, sweetheart."

"What dimension are you connecting to?" I felt foolish even asking the question, since I didn't know the names of any other dimensions. It all seemed like something from a science fiction book.

Fitz typed and pulled up the desert canyon landscape image I'd seen when we'd entered the room.

"Wait a minute," I scoffed. "You're not serious."

Rachel looked at me. "What is it, Bryce?"

I pointed to the screen. "Don't you recognize where that is?"

They stared at the screen until a flash of recognition filled Charlie's face. "Is that…"

Rachel saw it a moment later. "*Kingdom*?"

Fitz grinned. "Did you expect anything less?"

"What are you saying?" I turned to the silver machine next to us. "That your alternate dimension is a video game?"

"What if the answer was yes?" a voice boomed from behind us. We spun around to see an elderly Asian man standing several feet away. He supported his tall, thin frame with a cane, which made him seem frail, yet somehow his voice had been deep and strong.

Fitz scrambled to his feet. "Oh, Mr. Yao. I didn't see you there." The grin had disappeared from his face. Whoever this old man was, he seemed important. Another man stood two steps behind, like a personal assistant at the ready.

"Sit down," Mr. Yao ordered. Fitz sunk back into his chair, its supports groaning under his weight. Yao looked at us questioningly. "Well?"

"I'd say that was impossible," I replied to his question that still hung in the air. "There's no way to transport something from this world into a virtual dimension of a video game like *Kingdom*."

Yao laughed in a low clucking sound, like his tongue was sticking to the roof of his mouth and he was almost choking. He was taller than me, certainly over six feet, and while probably in his seventies, his eyes were alert and brimming with a fire.

"We're explorers, my young friends. You've heard it said that space is the final frontier, but that is such a limited view. New worlds exist far beyond our consciousness, past our physical dimension. Space exploration promised to be the next horizon, but we believe that our options are limitless if we utilize a micro digital propulsion that we call digital frontiering. We work here to construct a bridge to the virtual dimension."

I glanced at the satellite image on the screen and then back at Yao. "Into *Kingdom*? But why?"

"Even an enormous leap like this one must begin with a small step. Think of it as a test. Considered by some to be insignificant, perhaps, but it is a crack in the door to a world far beyond the physical constraints of this decaying planet."

He nodded at Fitz, and an image of Earth floating in space appeared on the wall. "Our measly planet is crumbling. Call it climate change or the start of a new geological age, but mankind is destined to go the way of the dinosaurs. We will be extinguished. For decades, scientists have assumed that our best route off this planet was a journey to a star system beyond our own.

"But what they failed to imagine—not surprisingly, since we've only recently found a path through dimensions—is the ability to create an entirely new world. One of our own making that we can both build and inhabit. We have the chance to be our own God, in a manner of speaking. For a new dawn, a second creation. Eden."

Charlie looked confused. "Eden?"

Yao seemed amused, his eyes narrowing. "Not enough…" He paused, searching for a phrase. "Sunday school in your youth, Mr. Kilroy?" He again made that odd clucking sound with his tongue. "Surely you've heard the Hebrew and Christian stories of how the Divine put man and woman in the garden at the dawn of creation? Of course, even the path of the Buddha speaks of a rebirth, a new beginning at the end of suffering. That is our goal here—to bring enlightenment and nirvana through a new world. A new beginning. A new Eden."

We stood silently, staring at the old man with this fantastical vision. Was he serious? Or a raving madman? The latter seemed more likely, but after everything I'd seen at this place, I wasn't so sure anymore.

Yao clapped his hands, waking us from our trance. "I've told you too much, too fast. I forget myself sometimes. My enthusiasm gets the better of me. You'll understand in due time."

Rachel found her voice. "What does this have to do with us?"

Yao smiled. "Why, you are to help build it, my dear." He waved his arm across the room. "They are all like you. The brightest minds of your generation brought together for a singular purpose—to increase the velocity of man's regeneration."

I bit my lip as I stared at the machine and then turned back to Yao. "Who are you?"

Yao broke into a loud cackle that seemed to fill the room.

It raised the hairs on the back of my neck. "I am the man who will bring all this to fruition, young Bryce. The man behind the curtain. He who moves the pieces on the board."

He reached out, grabbing my hand quickly, like the strike of a cobra. Dark veins bulged in his forearm as his bony fingers gripped my hand like a vice. "You can call me Mr. Yao. I am chairman of Liàngzǐ shìyě, although you'll be more familiar with our subsidiary gaming division named Q2. Having a ready fleet of programmers can serve many uses for an undertaking such as ours."

"It gives us an enormous advantage over the competition," Fitz chuckled from his chair.

Yao turned and shot Fitz an icy glare.

Fitz shrugged. "Such as they are."

Yao's assistant stepped forward and whispered in his ear.

Yao nodded. "I'm afraid I must leave you now." I could have been imagining things, but he seemed to be staring directly at me when he said, "I have great plans for you here. Our future—the new Eden—awaits."

CHAPTER TWELVE_

A fog enveloped the winding mountain roads as I headed home late Sunday afternoon. That seemed appropriate with my head in its own thick cloud, a near avalanche of conflicted thought—meeting Yao, the Eden Machine, Heather Avanair and Sturgis, working with Charlie and Rachel—there was too much to process. My chest constricted with each hairpin switchback down the mountain. I needed air.

I yanked the wheel and pulled into the parking lot of a scenic overlook. I leaped out of the car and breathed deep. What had I gotten myself into? Was it even real? All those people and machines and computers must do something, but it seemed more like a movie set, like it was all a giant mirage. I thought back to Yao's words in the lab, that we were on the cutting edge of a new digital frontier. What had he compared it to? The race into space against the Russians?

My phone shifted in my pocket. I'd forgotten to switch it on. I'd been so overwhelmed after winning the competition and hearing Yao's speech that I'd barely even said goodbye to Charlie and Rachel. We'd promised to stay in touch, but I didn't have their numbers. I could probably track them down, but I had the sense Q2 didn't want us speaking outside the compound. Heather had whisked us out to the front reception room where our bags were magically packed and waiting for us.

The phone powered up, and once it cycled for service, it showed nearly a dozen voice mails. I peered through slight holes in the fog at the valley far below. Somewhere down there was Milton, Mom and Dad, Zach, and Maggie, but I felt very far from home. Maybe this was simply what it felt like when you had to take responsibility for your own life and live on your own. But this was all so sudden. Was I even ready? They'd said I was special, a chosen one, but I'd never imagined anything like this would happen. Telling my parents seemed like the right thing to do, despite Q2's instructions. I went back to my car, but somehow I felt like things would never be the same.

* * *

Zach and Andrew were kicking a soccer ball in the front yard when I pulled up to the house around eight. It was just getting dark, but at the end of summer, days were long and warm.

Zach passed me the ball as I stepped from the Mustang. "Maggie's not happy with you."

"No?" I deftly trapped the ball and sent it toward Andrew. It had been a few years since I'd played soccer, focusing more on track in high school, but my old skills came back quickly.

"I think the word she used was 'pissed,'" said Andrew, always the smart aleck, passing the ball.

I stared him down for a second, then smiled and kicked him a hard pass. "Don't you have your own house to bother people at?"

Andrew was around nearly as much as Maggie was and had been Zach's best friend since the second grade. He lived with his mom and three older sisters. Since he almost never saw his dad, who lived out in San Antonio, ours tried to include him as much as possible. I think if I lived in a house with four females, I'd want to get out a lot too.

"She was trying to reach you," Zach said, passing the ball around our triangle formation. "But we told her we didn't know where you were."

I rolled my eyes. "Everyone knew I was camping with Tony. What's the big deal all of a sudden?"

"We just missed your coolness so much." Andrew laughed and kicked the ball back at my knee.

"Mom has a dinner plate saved for you," said Zach.

"Great." The lights were on inside the house, and I could see Mom moving back and forth in the kitchen. I'd texted from the overlook that I'd be home in a couple hours, and I'd built up enough trust over the years that my parents rarely worried about me getting in trouble. I thought about the lies I was now carrying around and tried to push away my guilt.

"Where's Dad?"

"He was watching the golf tournament." Zach nodded at the other side of the house. "But I think he's back in his office getting ready for a meeting tomorrow."

I worried that Dad was getting consumed by work. While I was growing up, he'd always had a solid paycheck with an understanding boss who'd trusted him. But when a venture capital fund acquired his company in a hostile takeover, they cleaned house. Most of the senior managers were sent packing, even people as experienced as Dad. At his new job, his boss Frank didn't seem to share that same level of trust. Dad politely called it a difference in management styles, but Frank just seemed like a jerk to me.

I grabbed the gear from my fake camping trip out of the trunk, with the new laptop from orientation hidden in the bottom of a duffel bag. I didn't want to explain why or how I had a new state-of-the-art laptop after a weekend in the woods with Tony. I'd already started thinking about hiding places in my room. Another of the many secrets I'd be keeping from everyone.

I set the duffel down when my phone buzzed. Maggie's smile filled the screen. "Hey there," I answered.

"You're alive!" Maggie's voice was playful, but her tone was the same as how Mom sounded when Dad watched too much golf.

"Fear not," I said. "Didn't you get my text?"

"I did, but I thought your kidnappers might have hacked your phone just to keep us off track. It's not like you to go dark for three days."

"Two and a half."

"Uh-huh."

I chuckled uncomfortably. "Sorry. Tony and I were out of cell range most of the time." I tried to redirect. "How was your weekend?"

"Eh, pretty slow, other than working yesterday. The rain washed out soccer practice Friday night. Did you get soaked at the campsite?"

I realized I'd been locked inside all weekend. I hadn't even looked out a window to see what the weather had been like. "It actually held off. Just a few sprinkles."

"You didn't get any of the rain?"

"Nope. Must have missed us up in the mountains."

"Well that was fortunate. It poured here."

Zach hit the side of my car with the soccer ball. I glared at him and grabbed the rest of the gear with my free hand. "Well, I'm just unloading the car. Can I call you later?"

"Okay. I missed you, Bryce."

"Missed you too. Bye."

I walked inside and got through conversations with Mom and Dad without serious blowback. They seemed to have no suspicions that I'd been off doing something secretive.

I returned the gear to the garage and then brought my bag to my room, searching for the best place to hide the laptop. Our old cat, White Sox, used to climb behind the drawers along the floor under my mattress. I pulled one out and reached my arm in as far as it could go. Sure enough, there was extra space past where the closed drawer rested. Once the laptop was secure in the compartment, I rolled the drawer back in without fear of crushing the computer. It was a bit cumbersome to get in and out, but as long as no one else removed the drawer, it would be a perfect hiding space.

A knock sounded behind me.

"Hey," Zach's voice called from the hallway.

I made sure the drawer was closed as he walked into the room.

"What's up?" I said, trying to sound casual from my position on the floor.

"Mom wants you to come get some food." He eyed me a second longer than usual. "You fall down?"

"Just unpacking." I did a few fast crunches and jumped up. "Where's Andrew?"

"We wanted to play another round of *Kingdom*, but Mom said we had to stay outside and get some exercise. Andrew's not much of a soccer player, so he called his sister to come pick him up." Zach glanced down the hall and then grinned at me. "Ya wanna play a quick round?"

I didn't know if I could look at *Kingdom* the same way anymore. What had once seemed like a fun diversion was now so much more. I buried all those feelings deep inside and away from Zach. There was no need for him to know. It was better for him to stay innocent. A part of me wished that I still was.

I tussled his hair as I stepped into the hall. "Sorry, gotta eat."

CHAPTER THIRTEEN_

Mom peppered me with questions about my weekend of camping and hiking with Tony, but I did a good job keeping her in the dark. I chatted with Dad about the highlights of the golf tournament and then excused myself to my room, claiming I was tired from fitful sleeping in the tent. I kept a call with Mags brief, promising to catch up more tomorrow.

As I got ready for bed, I opened my regular computer and considered the best way to find Charlie and Rachel. Charlie had said he lived in Edgarton, but I didn't think Rachel had mentioned her town, only that she'd visited Wickman. As I started searching social media and Google for them both, an email alert flashed on the corner of the screen. It was like the cryptic message that had held the original orientation invitation.

Message waiting. Please view on dedicated device.

I glanced behind me to make sure my bedroom door was closed, but then I got up and locked it, just in case Zach popped in again. I retrieved the new laptop from its hiding spot with another sensation of descending into the rabbit hole. I clicked on the waiting message, and a page of legal terms and conditions scrolled past on the screen before I was prompted to click on an acceptance box. I wondered if everything with Q2 would be so formal. Once again, my eyes glazed over as I tried to make sense of the language. I clicked on the "accept" button, and the screen changed.

A shorter message from Heather Avanair appeared. It was only a few brief sentences, but they were instructions for a programming sequence project due at nine the next morning. I scrolled lower, considering the assignment. Had Rachel and Charlie received something similar? Were we still working together, or was I now on my own? I glanced at the clock. It was already 10:00 PM. This was going to take all night.

Maybe it wasn't as bad as it looked. I breathed deeply and then jumped into it, meticulously working through the lines of code, trying to get my head around the project. Soon, I fell into a rhythm and my fingers were flying over the keys.

I WOKE TO A BEEPING. I'd fallen asleep at my desk. My back ached. I rubbed my eyes and looked at the clock. 3:00 AM. Last I remembered, I'd been programming. I turned back to the screen. A blinking interface emitted a tone every few seconds, prompting me to finish.

I yawned and scrolled further down the screen. The sections that needed coding kept going and going. I was never going to finish. But this was the first assignment. I couldn't stop now. Not after all I'd seen. Dad was always talking about making a good first impression. What if this was my big chance to prove I could perform on my own? I had to keep going. I rubbed my eyes again and started typing, trying to focus on the patterns. I could sleep later.

The sun was already streaming through my bedroom window as I clicked submit and closed the laptop. My spine was on fire. I stood and clasped my fingers, stretching my arms. I tried to remember what was happening today. Monday. I had work at the store through closing. And—oh, crap. I was supposed to be at midsummer track workouts by eight.

I looked at the clock and groaned. That was in twenty minutes. I was going to be late.

I FAKED a leg cramp fifteen minutes into track workouts and Coach Simmons seemed to buy it. I didn't know how much I'd slept after drifting off over my laptop, but it wasn't enough. I dragged like a zombie through the rest of the day at FarmWorks. A half hour before closing, I stood at the register, checking out Mrs. Janakowski. She was buying a bird feeder, the fancy kind that claimed to keep the squirrels off, although I doubted they worked, and an eighty-pound bag of water-softening salt.

I carried the salt to her car, and she thanked me as always. When she pulled away, the parking lot was empty except for my Mustang and another car I didn't recognize. I walked back in the front door and noticed a woman standing near the dog toys aisle. I hadn't seen her walk in.

"Let me know if you need any help," I called.

Heather Avanair turned around and smiled at me. My

heart nearly stopped. What was she doing here? Mags was meeting me for a late dinner after work. I glanced up at the clock over the register. She was supposed to be here in fifteen minutes, but she was always early.

Heather walked up the aisle to where I stood in front of the counter. "Hello, Bryce." Her words seemed to float through the air, steeped in her Australian accent.

"Hi," I managed to say, my mind suddenly fogged in, like I was still coming down the mountain. "What are you doing here?"

"Just checking in." She shot me a knowing glance. "Aren't you happy to see me?"

"What?" I forced a breath. "Sure, of course. Just surprised, that's all. I didn't expect you in Milton. Or at the store." I glanced over my shoulder out the front windows.

"Don't worry," said Heather. "I won't stay long. I don't want to complicate things with Maggie. At least not yet…"

My eyes bulged. Was she flirting with me or just playing with my head? "So, uh, why are you here then?"

She glanced at her phone, then back up at me. "I wanted to congratulate you for making it through the assessment process."

"I thought you already did that. Back at the compound."

She nodded. "Also, I wanted to say we were all very impressed by your work last night. I realize it must have seemed like a tight deadline, but part of what we look for in a candidate is someone who can prioritize the work above everything else. Dedication is important to Mr. Yao."

"Yeah, I noticed that."

"He's an amazing man," said Heather. "I also need to

remind you that everything you've learned about Eden is extremely confidential."

"Right, I know." Why was she telling me this again? They'd been over it like a hundred times, and every interaction seemed to start with signing something.

"The success and security of the project depends upon your discretion. But I know you understand that. Right, Bryce?"

Each time she said my name, a shiver went down my spine. And not an entirely unenjoyable one. I nodded, the roof of my mouth suddenly dry. "Yes," I managed to utter.

"Good." She flashed a killer smile, then placed a thin envelope in my hands. "For you."

"What's this?"

"Open it."

I peeled open the envelope and pulled out two pieces of glossy paper. I flipped them over. Tickets to see London Towers at the Civic Center in early September. Maggie and I had wanted to go, but the concert had sold out in less than ten minutes. I looked up at Heather. "Are you kidding? How did you know?"

She smiled. "We thoroughly research all of our recruits. Think of it as a reward."

"For what?"

"For a job well done, Bryce." She placed her hand on my arm. "This is only the beginning. Keep working hard, and there is more to come." She squeezed her fingers. "Much more."

Lights swept through the windows and over the shelves ahead of me. The sound of an engine turned off. I looked at the clock. Five minutes to seven. That had to be Maggie.

My heart was already beating quickly, but it seemed to kick up a notch. When I turned back, Heather was leaning over the counter and pulling two dog treats from the jar that sat beside the register. "I have a couple Rottweilers who would love these. I trust you can take care of it for me?"

I hurried around to the other side of the counter and rang up the sale. I'd put money in from my wallet later. I placed the treats in a small paper bag and handed it to Heather.

"Thank you, Bryce. We'll be in touch soon. Have a good night." She smiled at me one last time and then stepped away. She reached the door just as Maggie was entering.

Mags held the door open as Heather walked through. "Thank you," Heather called back as she moved into the night.

Maggie came toward me at the counter, still wearing her nametag. She'd come right from the dress shop. "Hi!" She glanced around to make sure the store was empty, then leaned across and kissed me. "I feel like you've been gone forever."

I tried to laugh normally. "Yeah." But my head was still spinning from speaking with Heather.

"What's that?" Maggie pointed to the tickets on the counter.

"What?" I'd forgotten they were still there, but she leaned closer and picked them up before I could react.

"Oh my god!" Her face filled with a gigantic smile. "Are these yours?"

I tried to adjust my face to match hers. "Surprise…"

She squealed and hugged me over the counter again. "How did you get these? I thought that show was sold out?"

"I, uh, bought them off Joey back in the warehouse. He couldn't use them and knew we were fans."

"Oh my god, it's going to be amazing!" She turned and

yelled at the door to the warehouse in the back of the store. "Thank you, Joey!"

I couldn't help but laugh as I walked around the counter. "He left an hour ago."

"Oh." Maggie nodded at the clock. "Well in that case, it's practically seven. Can you close up? I'm starving."

CHAPTER FOURTEEN_

The remaining weeks of summer were a blur. A tiring repetition of late-night assignments, grinding track workouts, and long hours at the store. I did my best to keep up appearances that everything was fine, but I was starting to crack. By Labor Day weekend, fears and secrets filled my mind and threatened to upend me. I'd always looked forward to my senior year of high school, but now as it lay just around the corner, everything felt wrong.

Maggie and I had joined a group of friends at the lake for the end of summer and the start of a new school year. The weather was hot, and splashing through the water with Mags in her bikini was plenty distracting, but life felt off. I was constantly on edge, as though I was waiting for someone unexpected to show up around every turn, or for all my secrets to leak out. The weekend passed with no messages, but I felt exhausted from always being on guard and constantly checking my phone for an email alert that the next programming assignment was waiting.

School started on Tuesday, sucking me in to the routine of classes and afternoon track practice. For a few hours, I almost convinced myself that the secret escapade up the mountain and the summer of late-night assignments had been imagined. Things felt normal. All my classmates' attention focused again on who was dating who, the upcoming big game against our crosstown rivals Central Catholic, and, of course, stressing about which colleges you were applying to and what you'd be doing after high school. It felt odd keeping the news that I'd secured a full scholarship from Maggie, but I stayed quiet. They'd made that instruction crystal clear, and I couldn't do anything to jeopardize the agreement. It was too important.

My cell phone rang as I walked to the athletic clubhouse for track practice after school. I answered, but whoever was on the other end had poor service. All I could hear was static. I hung up and then rang the number back.

It picked up quickly. "Go for Charlie."

"Charlie?" I said, only to hear a beep and realize that I'd reached a voice mail. I started over. "Hey Charlie, I think you just called me. How are you? I've been trying to look you up, but it seems you found me first. Have you heard from Rachel? Call me back. There's a lot I want to talk to you about."

I ended the call and joined some guys from the team who were walking into the locker room. As I closed my locker after changing, a message chimed on my phone. It was a text from the same number that had called before. Charlie.

Can't speak now but need to talk to you.

I quickly typed back. *Tonight?*

K. Watch ur back.

I stared at the phone. Watch my back? What did that mean?

"Bryce, get your ass out here if you want to run Thursday!" Coach Simmons bellowed from the hallway. "You can selfie with your sweetheart on your own time!"

I looked up from the phone, realizing the locker room was empty. "Coming, Coach!"

I tried to focus on practice, but I couldn't get my mind off of Charlie's message.

* * *

I DIDN'T KNOW what time Charlie wanted to talk that night, but I assumed it would be late. He had my number, so I waited for him to call. At dinner, family conversation centered on the first day of school.

"How are your teachers?" asked Dad.

I shrugged. "Pretty good. Maggie's in my civics class, although Mr. Bauer wouldn't let us sit next to each other."

"I have Mrs. Craig for Algebra," Zach moaned.

I grimaced. "Good luck. She's tough. Lots of homework."

"Great. At least I don't have any tonight." His lips curled into a smile. "Wanna play a round after dinner?"

"I have a lot of studying to do tonight, believe it or not," I answered.

Mom raised her eyebrows. "On the first day of school?"

"It's my senior year, Mom. I need to focus."

Dad passed the basket of rolls. "Don't argue with the boy, Trish. If he wants to study, let him."

"You're right," she said.

"I actually had a very good day," Dad announced, failing to hold back a smile.

"Really?" I said.

"Did you get fired?"

"Zach!" said Mom. "That's not funny."

My brother shrugged. "Well, I thought he didn't like this job. That would make it good news if he didn't have to do it anymore."

Dad shook his head. "No, I didn't get fired, thankfully. No matter how much I like or dislike it, we need the paycheck. And I don't dislike it, things just got off to a rocky start. But that might be changing."

We all stared at him, waiting, but he just took a bite of mashed potatoes.

"Well, don't leave us hanging, Dad," I said. "What happened?"

He wiped his mouth. "Sorry. Well, we've been doing a lot of marketing outreach lately for the new line, and today, I got a bite. A really big bite."

"A new client?" asked Zach.

Dad nodded. "It looks like it. The request came direct from their corporate headquarters in Omaha. Frank is quite excited about it."

Mom reached over and squeezed his hand. "That's wonderful, honey. You've been working so hard. We're all proud of you. Aren't we, boys?"

"Yeah, great job," I said.

"Nice going, Dad," added Zach. "That's definitely better than being fired."

"Thanks, guys." He looked at us around the table. "I know I've been a little on edge recently, and that you've had to make some sacrifices, which I truly appreciate."

"We're a team, Dad," I said, and then without thinking

added, "and I may have a lead on a scholarship. That would help too, right?"

Dad grinned. "That would help a lot, but either way, we'll be fine. I don't want you to feel pressure. Just do your best."

"Mr. Jenkins says pressure's just the air in your tires," said Zach.

Dad chuckled. "He may be onto something there."

I helped Zach clear the dishes, then retreated to my room with my backpack. I tried not to stare at my phone. Would Charlie even call?

Aside from his cryptic message about watching my back, I was looking forward to talking to him. It would be nice to compare notes. Was he working on the same project that I was, or had Heather assigned him something different? My batches of code were a small part of the bigger project. But if I was to believe Mr. Yao, Eden was a huge effort requiring the work of many programmers. Did they all have crazy schedules and deadlines like me?

I jumped when my phone beeped. But it wasn't a call from Charlie, it was another assignment alert email. My stomach churned in anticipation of another long night of coding. I locked my door and pulled the laptop from its hiding place. I plugged it in so the battery could recharge, then logged in with my fingerprint. The message flashed impatiently. I scanned through the instructions of another coding project, this one longer than the previous. Charlie still hadn't called, but maybe he'd become tied up with a similar assignment. I clasped my fingers, stretching, before I dug in at the keyboard.

* * *

I CRUMPLED THE SODA CAN, lining it up on my windowsill next to the other three. It had taken all night, but I'd finished. Finally. I submitted the files for encryption, sending them off across the web for review from who knows who back up on the mountain. I laid my head on my arms and closed my eyes, drifting to sleep at the desk.

In my dreams, I saw workers by the dozen, feeding my code into the Eden Machine like wood chips. Yao sat in his luxury box, cackling with his odd clucking sound. He spoke to me, but it wasn't his voice I heard. It was the desperate guy who'd called to me through the vent. He said I had to contact Tyler and send him codes. Project Joshua.

My vision exploded, and I was inside *Kingdom* staring across multiple landscapes, hunting clues, evading Rangers.

I jerked awake at my alarm clock's beeping. I was still at my desk, drool running down my arm. I'd barely slept, but I pulled my stiff body from the chair, wandering to the bathroom and cursing the project. I hoped a shower might wake me up enough to get through school.

Mr. Atkinson called me up to his desk at the end of class. I'd fallen asleep in the middle of Advanced Calculus. Normally Atkinson would pelt whiteboard erasers at kids who slept in his class, but it was such unusual behavior for me, he looked more concerned than upset.

I lied and said I was just worn out from pushing it too hard at track practice. I promised it wouldn't happen again, and he seemed to buy it. I didn't want to be lying to my teachers, but I certainly couldn't tell them the truth. Even if anyone suspected something was up, there was no way they'd ever guess what was really going on.

My phone buzzed when I was in the parking lot after the last bell. A text from Charlie.

Meet me at the old Milton water tower - tonight 10PM.

And B Careful.

CHAPTER FIFTEEN_

I knew the place, of course. Dad used to take Zach and me fishing at the small pond next to the VFW Hall on Route 60, just past the turnoff for the old water tower. I remembered riding my bike up the trail to see it once with Mike Kopeck in eighth grade. The tower had been abandoned since before I was born, I think. Dad said the town shut it down when they updated the water supply system and started using the Northside Reservoir across the valley for drinking water. Even then, the old basin had been rusting and creating unsafe particles in the water.

What I couldn't guess was how Charlie knew about the water tower, or what he was doing in Milton. Edgarton was on the other side of the mountain. It had to be a three-hour drive. And what was I supposed to be careful about?

I claimed I was running over to Maggie's to share some notes from civics class. Mom groused about it being too late, but I told her I wouldn't be long. The truth was, I had no idea how long I'd be or what Charlie wanted. What could he say at such a remote location that he couldn't say at a coffee shop?

I drove slowly up the dirt path. Potholes the size of basketballs would wreck my suspension if the car hit them too fast, and my Mustang had enough problems already. Low branches brushed against my windshield, and I hoped they weren't scratching the paint. The old car wasn't fancy, but it was all I had and it meant a lot to me. Ordinarily I'd never drive it down such a mess of a road, but something told me whatever Charlie needed to talk about was important.

I rolled to a stop where the trail dead-ended. My headlights caught the bumper of a green, rusted-out station wagon, pulled into the edge of the woods. I assumed it was Charlie's, but from its condition, the wagon could also have been sitting there for months.

Maybe this wasn't the safest place to be after dark, but it was a little late for that decision. I killed the engine. It took a moment for my eyes to adjust to the darkness, but soon I made out the dark outline of the metal tower's supports rising into the sky. A half moon provided just enough light to frame the old water basin, looming over the trees like some alien spaceship.

Tree frogs from the fishing pond sang out in the night like an orchestra. I stepped toward the car at the base of the tower and heard something drop into the leaves. I spun toward the sound, my heart thumping.

"Charlie?"

What would I do if it wasn't him? Maybe the car belonged to some deranged drifter, sleeping off too many drinks before adding another poor unsuspecting teenager to his list of victims. Or maybe the sound had been made by a bear, like the ones Dad warned us about on our camping trips along the Snake River. Would they wander this far down into the valley?

I glanced back at my car, wishing I'd brought some form of protection. I leaned over and felt around my feet, picking up a stick. It was too small to do any real damage, but somehow just holding something helped my confidence. I stepped toward the tower, squinting through the darkness. "Charlie, is that you?" I called again.

A light flashed above me.

"Bryce! Up here."

The light had come from the platform that circled the base of the water container. "Charlie?" I hissed. "What are you doing up there?"

"Climb the ladder," he called back. "It's safe, I promise."

I used my phone's light to inspect the ladder's rusted metal rungs. This was stupid, but I couldn't leave now. I pulled on the metal, placing my foot on the bottom rung to test its strength. It seemed secure. I gritted my teeth and slowly began to climb.

I'd never been particularly scared of heights, but I still didn't look down. I don't know how many feet off the ground that platform was, but it felt like I was climbing forever before my head poked through the opening to the platform. Charlie reached down and helped me onto the landing.

"Thanks for coming, Bryce."

I stared over the edge. At that height, I could see far and wide, even in the darkness. Just past the Mustang in the trees was the shadow of a small fenced-off power substation, some more trees, a housing development, and then all of Milton in the distance.

"Why couldn't we just talk down there?" I turned and looked at him. His hair was a mess and his eyes were bloodshot, like he hadn't slept for days or was on something. "What's the matter with you?" I asked.

"Keep your voice down." His eyes darted back and forth, watching the treetops as if he expected a giant bird to swoop down and carry him away. "I can't stay long."

I'd only known Charlie a short time, but his behavior now was so different from the happy-go-lucky guy I'd met at orientation. He didn't seem like the same person. "What are you talking about? What's happened to you?"

He stopped fidgeting and stared at me. "Have you been getting the assignments? The coding sequences on the laptops they gave us?"

"Yeah."

"Can you finish them?"

"It's been taking me practically all night," I answered, "but I've gotten them done."

Charlie nodded fast. "Right, all night. Me too. But it's too much, man. I can't do it anymore."

"Too much what? Too much work?"

He stared at me with his bloodshot eyes. "Too many codes, Bryce. They never stop. I can't keep up; it's ruining my life. I don't sleep. They just keep coming, day after day. I'm missing class. My grandma thinks I'm using again. I've lost weight. I can't eat…I think I'm going over the edge, man."

I glanced back at the ground and suddenly wondered if the reason he'd wanted to meet up here was because he planned to jump. "Have you spoken to Heather? Did you tell her you needed a break?"

"Heather? You mean Dr. Avanair?" Charlie laughed like I'd made a joke. "Oh, I tried to talk with the ice queen, but she wouldn't listen. She just threatened to kick me out of the program, rescind the scholarship offer, even sue my family."

I tried to imagine Heather saying something like that. It didn't fit the woman I'd met. I almost asked if he'd received a reward, like the tickets for next week's concert, but it was clear he'd had a much different experience than I had. But why?

"Have you heard from Rachel?" I asked.

"No. You?"

I shook my head. "I didn't even know how to reach you. How did you find me, anyway?"

Charlie grunted. "I'm pretty good at digging, but you weren't exactly hard to find. What are you, like, *Mr. Milton* or something? I'm surprised they don't have a statue of you outside your school."

I didn't know what to say to that, but he kept talking.

"That's not all I found, either."

"What else?" I asked.

He glanced back and forth again nervously. "I looked into Q2, Yao, the whole thing. Something's not right. Did you know that Ji Yao is a Chinese billionaire?"

I shook my head. I didn't, but I supposed the head of a huge computer company must have a lot of money. "So what?"

"It turns out that the U.S. government has been investigating Q2 and its holding company, Yang She, for all sorts of illegal activities, including human trafficking, tax evasion, and unfair trade practices. He's not a good dude, Bryce."

"Okay, he's a bad guy, but what does that have to do with us?"

He glanced around again like someone was listening.

"Remember that guy they dragged out of his room in the middle of the night?"

I nodded, thinking back to how the voice called to me through the vent.

"I did some checking into that too. There've been four missing kids that match our profiles in the last twelve months. All high school juniors or seniors. All top performers in their classes with plans to attend college for computer programming."

I stared back at him now. The night was muggy, but he was sweating like he'd been running for miles. "Are you sure? I think we'd have heard about that."

"I'm sure. The disappearances are spread across several states, but all lived close to the borders, and all were within driving distance of Tech's evil neighbor."

"And you think the guy they dragged away is one of those missing kids? How could you possibly know that?"

"Did he say anything to you?" Charlie asked. "You were in the next room, right?"

I shook my head. I'd never told Charlie or Rachel what had been said through the vent. I wasn't sure why. Probably because it sounded crazy, but maybe there was another reason. Maybe I didn't want it to be true. I would call Heather. Surely she'd have an explanation for all this.

I put my hand on Charlie's shoulder. "Avanair seems to like me. Let me talk with her. Maybe I can straighten all this out."

Charlie shook his head like they'd already defeated him. "It might be too late."

The rotors of a helicopter sounded in the distance. The

noise was far away, but Charlie ducked down like the copter was dive-bombing us.

I grabbed the metal rail tightly for balance. "It's okay, man. No one's coming for you."

He stood and stepped to the platform edge. "I wish you were right, Bryce." For a moment, I thought he really might jump, but he just stretched his foot down to the ladder. "I've gotta go."

I followed him down to the ground. "Are you going to be all right? When will I talk to you again?"

"I don't know," he answered, opening his car door. "But remember, Bryce..." He paused, staring back up at the water tower as if it might crash down on us any second.

"Yeah?"

"Watch your back."

CHAPTER SIXTEEN_

Several days went by, but I couldn't stop thinking about Charlie and what he'd said. While he'd looked and sounded crazy, some of his points rang true. But there had to be an explanation. Maybe the late nights and lack of sleep had worn him down. Some people handle pressure and deadlines better than others.

I hadn't received an assignment, but I pulled out the Q2 laptop and logged in anyway. I messaged Heather Avanair, asking her to contact me. I didn't really know what I would say, but I needed to help Charlie. If they knew he was so close to the edge, maybe they could back off on his workload for a while.

I'd barely hit submit on the secured messaging platform when my cell rang. The number was blocked, but I knew it wasn't a coincidence. Nothing I'd experienced with Q2 seemed to happen by accident.

I accepted the call, but the line had a strange, electronic tint. "Hello?" I said.

"Bryce," a voice answered. It was Heather, but her accent

sounded bent, like it was being filtered through a scrambling mechanism or routed around the world off of multiple satellites to avoid detection.

"Heather?"

"Yes. What's the problem?"

This was moving faster than I'd prepared for. "I, uh, I wanted to check in with you."

"Check in? About what? We haven't sent you a new assignment. Is something wrong?"

I decided just to say it. "It's about Charlie."

The line was silent for several seconds.

"Hello?" I finally said.

"What about him?" asked Heather.

"Well, he seems like he's having a really hard time with things."

"Did he contact you?"

I couldn't think of a lie that would make sense, since I had brought him up. "Yes, he came to see me."

"In Milton?"

"Right."

"When was this?"

I felt like she'd hooked me back up to the polygraph machine. "A couple nights ago."

"And what exactly did he say to you?"

"Well, he seemed really strung out, like he hadn't been sleeping and was cracking under the pressure. I told him I'd speak to you. I thought maybe if you could hold off giving him any new—"

"There's no need for you to be concerned about it, Bryce," she interrupted. "If Mr. Kilroy needs something, he should speak to us directly. Moving forward, you're not to have any contact with the other recruits, is that clear?"

What? Where was the flirtatious woman who'd showered me with praise and free concert tickets?

"Bryce, do you understand what I'm saying?" Heather asked again.

"Yes, I understand."

"Good. Please keep watch for additional assignments. You're doing great, Bryce," she added, her tone softening. "But keep focused on the task at hand, and let us worry about the rest, okay?"

I didn't know what choice I had other than to agree. "Yeah. Okay."

"Good night, Bryce." Then the line went dead.

I sat wondering what had just happened. Why was she so abrupt and closed? Charlie hadn't start acting nuts for no reason. He'd said he'd found information about Yao and Q2. Maybe I could do the same. I had to do something.

I logged off the silver laptop, placed it back behind the drawer, and then used my personal computer to search for everything I could think of related to the work at Q2—quantum physics, *Final Kingdom*, digital frontiering, Ji Yao, Johannes Sturgis, and the name Tyler. The results fed back a long list, but nothing seemed to fit, until I clicked down into sub-pages. There something caught my eye. It was a *Wall Street Journal* article from earlier in the year. Highlighted in the summary was a name that I immediately recognized. *Dr. William Hendrickson, Professor of Computer Science and Digital Propulsion.*

I remembered the odd conversation during my tour at Tech.

Was he working on projects similar to Sturgis and Q2? Their locations were certainly near one another. Could they be working together, or were they competitors? Mr. Torres in my Business Concepts class last year told us that sometimes competitors spring up in the same region, a result of partnership splits or of poaching of employees and ideas. That could be the case here, but it didn't fit with the message from the voice in the darkness. He hadn't asked me to reach out to Dr. Hendrickson—I'd have recognized that name immediately. He'd told me to contact someone named Tyler. Could he be at Tech too?

I ran another search for the Department of Computer Science at Tech and the name "Tyler." A hit came up near the top of the second results page. *Tyler Barnes, Graduate Assistant, Department of Computer Science.* Bingo. That had to be it. Tyler Barnes. But what would I even say if I contacted him?

For a moment, I considered whether I was being monitored by Q2. There was no doubt they were connected to the silver laptop, but could they hack my personal computer too? The invitation seemed to have been a one-time message. Heather knew I liked London Towers, but that wouldn't have been very hard to figure out—they were half of Milton High's favorite band too.

I thought back to Charlie's warning about the hidden cameras in the sprinkler heads. My bedroom ceiling was empty of sprinklers, and the nearest smoke detector was out in the hallway. I stood, recalling the scenes on TV and movies where someone's house was bugged. I glanced under the lampshade by my nightstand and peered into the air-conditioning vent, but I didn't see any monitoring devices. Not that I'd recognize one if I saw it.

I decided it was worth the risk, and searched the

student/faculty directory on Tech's website. There it was —*Barnes, Tyler*. The name linked to an email address. I clicked it to open a blank message. What should I say? I decided to keep it simple and make it relevant to my Tech visit.

Subject: Looking for a connection

Dear Tyler,

Hello. I'm a high school senior and prospective freshman next year at Tech in the computer science department. I met Dr. Hendrickson briefly on my visit several weeks back, but an acquaintance of mine suggested I reach out to you directly. I have some questions about the program that I'm hoping you could answer.

Thanks, and I look forward to hearing from you soon.

Sincerely,

Bryce Pearson.

I read through the note a second time, making sure it was vague, but didn't sound too ridiculous. I figured that if Heather found it, I could innocently claim that I was just looking for more information about Tech's program. Q2 scholarship or not, I still hoped to enroll at Tech next fall. I sent the message and tried to put it out of my mind.

I CHECKED my computer the next morning before I got in the shower, but there was no reply. I dressed and met Dad at the breakfast table. He was wearing a tie, which even at his new job was unusual.

"Looking sharp," I said as he placed a stack of folders into his work bag.

"Thanks, son."

"You're not going on another job interview, are you?"

Dad chuckled. "No, thankfully I think those days are behind me." He rapped on the wooden table for good luck. "Frank and I have a big meeting this afternoon in Omaha. It's with the president of that company I told you about. If things go well, I could reach half my quota for the year."

I whistled. "Nice."

A horn sounded in the driveway, and Dad pulled the bag over his shoulder. "That's the car service. I've gotta go." He gave me a quick one-armed hug. "Sorry I won't make the meet today. Run strong."

"Will do. And good luck!" I poured a bowl of cereal as he walked down the driveway. His comment made me regret not working harder for the track meet. With everything else going on, I hadn't been taking my training as seriously as I should. So far Coach was cutting me some slack, but his patience would only last so long. I needed to buckle down.

An alert buzzed on my phone. A reply from Tyler. I froze mid-bite as I opened it.

Re: Looking for a connection

Dear Bryce,

Thanks for your email. I'm glad to hear you're considering the computer science program at Tech. Dr. Hendrickson actually mentioned to me he'd spoken with you. I'd be happy to answer any questions you may have. For ease of use, you can reach me via my secure personal messaging link below.

Tyler

I saw a link at the bottom of the message to a secure encryption site that advertised in computing magazines. It seemed over the top for a simple introduction email, but maybe it was standard procedure for the department. I hurried back to my room without finishing breakfast and opened the link on my computer. A padlock icon filled the corner of the screen, indicating that the message was encrypted.

I typed quickly. I only had a few minutes until Maggie was expecting me to pick her up for school.

Re: Looking for a connection

Tyler,

This might sound like an odd question, but I'm wondering what you know about the area of digital frontiering. My acquaintance is in the field and suggested I contact you. If this is an area of interest for you, perhaps we can meet. I've recently been introduced to this concept and have lots of questions.

Thanks,

Bryce

I hesitated over the send button, but a text buzzed on my phone.

Still picking me up?

Shoot, I was late again. I didn't think any longer, I just hit "Send" and bolted out the door. Halfway to the car, I remembered I needed my track uniform for the meet that afternoon and had to race back in to grab it. By the time I pulled into Maggie's driveway and she hopped in next to me in the front seat, the message to Tyler had completely left my mind.

CHAPTER SEVENTEEN_

Despite Heather's instructions, I had to try to talk to Charlie again. Dr. Avanair saying that she'd take care of it didn't leave me feeling very confident that he would be okay. I tried Charlie's number after class on the way to track and again on the way home from the meet. After going straight to voice mail the third time, I was officially worried, but didn't know what more I could do.

The next evening was the London Towers concert at the Civic Center Pavilion in Mercer, the next town over. Mags had been talking about little else for the past week as we geared up for the show. Tons of kids from school seemed to have somehow scored tickets, and it was being hyped as one big party. The weather was a perfect Indian summer evening for the outdoor concert.

I picked Maggie up around six so we'd have plenty of time to get parked and settled. When I arrived at her house, I opened the door on her side of the car and admired her walking down the porch as she waved goodbye to her parents. She looked gorgeous in a pair of just-short-enough denim cutoffs, a pink tank top, and with her long hair pulled into a ponytail.

She laughed as I walked around to open her door. "What are you grinning at?"

"You look good," I replied.

"Thanks." She leaned up and kissed me. "I'm excited for the show. Did you bring chairs?"

I nodded at the trunk. "Check."

She scrunched her shoulders together and squeaked in excitement. "This is going to be great. You have to thank Joey again for me."

"Who?" I asked, as I backed down the driveway.

"Joey. At the store. Didn't you say that's who you bought the tickets from?"

"Oh, right," I mumbled, remembering my lie. "I already thanked him." It would have been so much easier if I could say I'd received the tickets from Heather, but that would open a whole can of worms. I'd never be able to explain without telling her everything.

Maggie leaned back and looked through the sunroof. "Well, this is just a perfect evening." She grabbed my right arm and pulled it tight to her. "With the perfect guy."

"You're not so bad yourself."

By the time we parked and got through security, it was close to seven. We arranged our camp chairs in a row with our friends, midway across the terraced lawn of the outdoor amphitheater. We were sheltered under the pavilion roof, but the sky was clear as the sun faded over the horizon. The first opening act, an acoustic female singer from Ireland, was just walking onto the stage.

"Look, there's Liv and Jordan," said Maggie, pointing several rows ahead of us. "I have to say hi."

"Okay, I'm going to get some food," I replied. "Do you want anything?"

Maggie shook her head. "Maybe just a water right now. Thanks." She gave me a quick kiss and stepped away. I waved to Jordan and then headed for the long rows of concession tents along the road behind the pavilion.

The gentle strumming of the Irish singer on the stage mixed with the buzz of the crowd. It was just as Mags had said, a perfect night to be outside for a concert. I tried to relax and enjoy the moment. Lately it seemed like everything was moving a hundred miles per hour. Tonight, things felt more like normal, like what a typical high schooler should do, instead of having secret tasks to complete for dubious Chinese tech companies.

I thought about the tickets. It felt good to have Heather compliment my coding. There wasn't anything illegal or even unethical about her giving them to me. I'd worked hard throughout the night to get that assignment done. I deserved a reward. So why did it feel so weird? Had Heather just randomly dropped by with tickets, or did she know that Maggie was about to arrive? Did she time her visit purposefully to ramp up my stress level? Maybe I was just paranoid. Lack of sleep will do that.

I scanned the menu board hanging over the burger and fries counter. I tried to get a look at the food the guy and girl at the front of the line were carrying away, but as they turned around, the dark-haired girl looked up. It was Rachel.

Our eyes met, registering similar surprised responses. "Bryce? What are you doing here?" She stepped forward and gave me a hug, then retreated somewhat awkwardly and nodded to the guy next to her, who I assumed was her boyfriend. "Oh, Adam, this is my friend Bryce."

Adam didn't look particularly happy that Rachel had hugged me, but he faked a smile and shifted his food tray so he could shake my hand.

"Nice to meet you," I said.

"How do you two know each other?" Adam asked.

I froze up at the question. I hadn't expected to see Rachel at the concert and certainly hadn't practiced an explanation for how we knew each other.

Thankfully, Rachel was quicker on her feet. "We met on a prospective student tour at Wickman."

If I hadn't known better, I would have thought she was telling the truth. I just hoped Adam didn't ask me anything about the college I'd never visited.

But he didn't. Adam nodded and looked back toward the stage. "Well, I'm going to bring this food to our seats." He looked back at me with a glance that said "don't talk to her too long," but out loud he only said, "Nice to meet you, Bryce."

"I'll be right there," Rachel assured him, but when Adam was out of earshot, she turned back to me excitedly. "How are you?"

"I'm good," I answered. "You're a *Towers* fan, too?"

She laughed. "Who isn't? But actually, I, uh…" She paused awkwardly, like she was battling her fake storyline.

"It's okay," I said quickly. "I got mine from Dr. Avanair. You too?"

"Oh, thank god!" She exhaled loudly. "Yes, she gave them to me. But it's so terrible not being able to tell anyone! I hate lying to Adam. Is it the same for you?"

I nodded. "Yeah. Maggie thinks I bought them from a guy at work." At the mention of her name, I glanced over my shoulder, suddenly self-conscious about talking with Rachel. I could try the same story that Rachel had given Adam, but Maggie had been with me at Tech, and she knew I hadn't visited Wickman.

"I've been wanting to reach out to you," said Rachel, "but I didn't know how. Have you heard from Charlie?"

"He came to see me last week in Milton, but he looked terrible. He's not sleeping, and he's paranoid that they're following him. I'm worried about him, but he won't answer his phone."

"*Are* they following him?" Rachel turned and scanned the crowd. "Following us?"

I was quiet for a moment, sorting out her question from the music. "I don't know."

We talked for a few more minutes, comparing notes about our programming assignments. We seemed to be working on similar coding sequences, and like me, she was staying up till all hours just to get them done.

"But I don't know how much longer I can keep it up," said Rachel. "My mom's getting suspicious."

I told her about Charlie's conspiracy theories from his research into Q2 and Yao. "He thinks they're up to something sinister, but I don't know what to think."

"Me neither." She glanced over my shoulder at the stage, as the singer ramped up into a faster song. "I need to get going. Adam's not the jealous type, but he's going to wonder what happened to me."

I thought again of Maggie. "Yeah, me too. Let's stay in

touch, okay?" I gave her my number, and we promised to talk soon.

We hugged goodbye, but she stopped short as she started to walk away. "Wait! What are we going to do about Charlie?" she called back.

I shrugged. "I don't know what we can do."

"We should go check on him."

"Where?"

"Why not at his house?"

I thought back to where he said he lived. On the other side of the mountain. "Edgarton's kind of a ways."

"We can go Monday," she said. "It would be too hard to explain where I've been going on a Sunday."

I raised my eyebrows. "Monday? I have school."

"Can't you skip it? If we leave in the morning, we can get back home by the time school's over. It will be the perfect cover. You can pick me up on the way."

I thought through her idea. "I guess we could do that."

Rachel's face turned pleading. "It's for Charlie. You know he'd do the same for us."

CHAPTER EIGHTEEN_

I left the house Monday morning at the normal time for school, working hard to keep my lies straight about why I couldn't pick up Zach at the end of the day and why I wouldn't see Maggie in class. Sneaking off seemed so much easier on TV. But eventually I was driving out of Milton toward Rachel's house, two counties over in Limerick.

Part of me felt nuts, cutting school to find Charlie's house way up in Edgarton. I'd been to the town once for a preseason regional track meet sophomore year, and I thought Mom's great-aunt lived there in a nursing home. Most of the town was built around the remains of an old mining village, but like many small towns around the country, Main Street had more "For Sale" signs and boarded-up buildings than open storefronts.

We stopped at Edgarton High first. It stood to reason that Charlie should be in class in the middle of the day, but I think both of us suspected otherwise.

"I'm afraid Charles isn't here," said the woman behind the counter at the school's office. Her name was Carol, based on the nameplate on the empty desk behind her. "It's not like him to miss class, either. He's one of our best students."

"Is he sick?" I asked.

She nodded. "There's a stomach bug going around. He's been out the last two days."

This was what we were afraid of. I realized we had no idea where he lived, but before I could reply, Rachel took things in her own hands.

"That's too bad," she began. "We're both student ambassadors from UCLA, and we were really hoping to meet with Charles about a potential scholarship in our computer sciences department."

My mouth dropped open, but Carol didn't seem to notice. Her eyes lit up in amazement at Rachel's story. "You mean, you've come all the way from California?"

Rachel nodded. "We think he could be a wonderful asset to our university, but without a personal interview, we'd have to move on to the next scholarship candidate."

She was really laying it on thick, but it seemed to be working.

"Oh my goodness," stammered Carol. "A scholarship would be such a blessing." She looked up at us sadly. "That family has had such a tough time."

"Carol," I said, in my most trustworthy voice, "it would be so helpful if you could share his home address. We'd love to swing by after coming all this way."

Poor Carol looked like she might have a stroke as she weighed the curveball we'd thrown at her. She glanced over her shoulder at the office behind her with *Principal* above the door. She bit her lip, looked back at us, then lifted an oversized index card box from her desk. She pulled a card, which I assumed was Charlie's record, then placed it flat on the counter, sliding it stealthily toward me.

I clicked a quick picture with my phone and slid it back to her. "You're a lifesaver, Carol," I whispered.

"Thank you so much," said Rachel.

"Fingers crossed!" Carol called, suddenly throwing caution to the wind, with her hand up in the air as we walked out of the office.

We broke down laughing once we were around the corner in the parking lot. "That was incredible!" I said. "Where did you come up with that?"

Rachel grinned. "I don't know, we needed to do something. And you weren't so bad yourself." Then her smile faded as she focused back on our goal. "I just hope he's okay."

"Yeah," I said. "It's a bad sign that he's been out of school."

We typed the address into my GPS and followed the directions into the countryside a few miles outside of town. I rolled to a stop at a quiet intersection. The road turned left, but the GPS said to go right onto little more than a gravel lane and a telephone line darting between the trees on rickety poles.

"You think this is the way?"

"It says Ledbetter Lane," said Rachel. "I had no idea he lived this far into the country."

I pulled onto the narrow road, my tires spinning briefly on the loose gravel. I wondered how Charlie could learn how to code and have computer access to play enough *Kingdom* for Q2 to notice him living way out here, but I supposed they could still have broadband, or maybe he played at a friend's house or the library.

We bounced along the dirt road for another quarter mile until we came to a wooden house, set back from the road on the left. Its bare, plank siding was screaming out for paint, but mounted to the roof, in stark contrast, was a shiny satellite dish. That must be Charlie's web access.

Rachel pointed at a rusted mailbox along the road. "Kilroy" was painted on the side in faded red letters.

"I guess this is the place." I eased onto the end of the driveway and killed the engine. "What exactly are we going to do here again?" We'd talked about it on the drive up, but it still seemed sketchy.

"See if he's here, for one thing. And if he's not, see what might have happened." Rachel opened the car door. "Just follow my lead."

We walked along the weed-covered dirt drive toward the house, passing beat-up cars that hadn't seen the road for years. An assortment of plastic toys and rusted bikes were scattered around the front lawn, but I didn't see any little kids. Maybe Charlie had younger brothers and sisters who were at school.

The porch creaked ominously as I placed a hesitant foot on the first step. There didn't seem to be a bell, so Rachel knocked gently on the cracking wood frame of the door.

I glanced back at the cars taking permanent residence in the driveway. "Maybe no one's home."

"Help you?"

We turned to see a woman standing in the grass by the corner of the house. She was wearing a green jogging suit that was a couple sizes too small for her large build. Gray streaks ran through her dark hair, but I couldn't tell whether she was Charlie's mom or grandmother. She leaned against the house with her leg propped on the kind of wheeled cart that people use in place of crutches. I looked closer and realized her right foot was in a cast.

Rachel stepped off the porch toward her. "Mrs. Kilroy?"

The woman cackled like she'd heard a joke. "Ain't been Mrs. Kilroy in years. The name's Jennette."

I followed Rachel into the yard. "Does Charlie live here?"

Jennette crossed her arms. "Maybe. Depends on who's askin'."

Rachel gave a friendly smile. "We're friends of his."

"Ain't never seen you two 'round here before." Jennette looked at my car in the driveway. "You from Edgarton? Why aren't you in school?"

Her voice slurred slightly, and I wondered if she'd been drinking.

Rachel shook her head. "No, I'm from Limerick. And we have today off from school, it's a teacher in-service day."

The woman, who I decided must be Charlie's grandma, lit a cigarette. She took a long drag and blew a cloud of smoke in our direction. I tried not to cough.

"Limerick, huh? Always thought that was an odd name for a town. What you want with my Charlie?"

I decided I needed to jump in. "I've been trying to call him, but he hasn't answered. And his school said he was home sick. Is he here?"

She glanced around, like Charlie might be sitting in one of the lawn chairs and we just hadn't noticed. "Don't see him."

"Do you know where he went?" asked Rachel. "We really need to speak with him."

Jennette scooted her cart toward us, her face wincing in pain as the wheels bumped along the uneven yard. "Last I saw Charlie was day before yesterday. Said he was goin' over to his cousin's place in town. He does that sometimes. It's where they play their video games and other nonsense after school."

She stopped next to a cracked plastic chair and eased herself carefully into the seat. She took another drag on her cigarette and looked up at us. “Lord knows he would stay on those games and that computer of his 24/7, if he could. You’d think he’d come around to help his poor Nana get along, but no, he’s much too busy. Good for nothing smart-ass. I told those other men the same thing, but they didn’t seem to care much.”

Our ears perked up. “What other men?” asked Rachel.

Jennette waved her hand like she was swatting at mosquitoes. “The ones from the electronics store. They came by here the other day and wanted to talk to Charlie. Said they needed to update something on one of his Internets. I asked ’em if they could help me with the reception of my dish up there. It’s supposed to be HD, you know, but it’s been fuzzy for weeks, and not just when it’s rainin’.”

She looked at me expectantly. “You know anything about satellite dishes?”

“Sorry,” I said, knowing we needed to get out of there. It wasn’t hard to figure out that the electronic store guys weren’t from Best Buy. I’d bet the Mustang that Heather or Sturgis, or maybe even Yao himself, had sent them.

Rachel seemed to think similarly. We made eye contact, and I nodded. “Well, if he comes home, please tell him that Rachel and Bryce were looking for him. Will you do that?”

Jennette nodded, but she was looking out across the yard, like something interesting was in the grass. I tugged on Rachel’s sleeve, and we turned for the car.

“That’s horrible,” Rachel whispered, as I started the engine and backed onto the gravel road. “I can’t believe Charlie lives there. Do you really think they took him?”

There was no reason to mince words. "Sounds that way."

"Just like the guy in the middle of the night at orientation. What's wrong with these people? Why would they recruit kids to work for them, act like it's some great opportunity, and then one by one, drag them away from their families?"

"We don't know if they do that to everyone," I said rather unconvincingly. "We're still here."

"For now." She seemed about to burst into tears.

I stopped the car at the end of the gravel road and turned toward her. "Hang on now. We don't know what happened. Maybe he really is over at his cousin's house playing video games."

Rachel looked at me skeptically. "You know that's not true."

"It could be."

"Then why hasn't he answered your calls?"

I shrugged, realizing my hopes were unlikely. "I don't know."

She let out a long breath and looked at her phone. "It's getting late. We need to head out if we're both going to get home in time."

I looked at the clock on the dash and nodded, accelerating onto the blacktop. I knew I needed to tell her about Tyler. While I didn't know Rachel well, I sensed that I could trust her. We were both in too deep for me to keep everything to myself. There'd been too many lies, too many secrets.

"There's something you need to know," I started. Then I told her everything. About the message from the voice through the vent, about Charlie's claims that Yao was suspected of various crimes, and finally, how I'd found Tyler Barnes and messaged him about digital frontiering.

When I finished, Rachel still sat quietly in the passenger seat. I couldn't tell if she was angry or just thinking. Maybe a mixture of both. "Do you really think this Tyler person can help us?" she finally asked.

"I hope so. I don't know where else we can turn."

She shook her head. "How could I have been so stupid? I never should have gone up there in the first place. Or signed all those papers, or kept all this from my mom. What was I thinking?"

I put my hand on her shoulder. "There was no way to know. If it makes you feel better, you're not the only idiot in the car. I was just as stupid."

Rachel shifted in her seat and I moved my hand away. "It doesn't. We should have been more cautious." She pointed to a green highway sign up ahead. It marked the exit for Tech and the road that cut up over the mountain. "Maybe we should go up there. Try to talk to him."

"Yao?"

"No, Tyler. You said he's at Tech, right?"

"Yeah, but I haven't heard back from him. I need to make sure he's someone we can trust." I leaned forward, staring at the base of the mountain. Somewhere far above us was Q2, the Eden Machine, and maybe Charlie. But all I wanted to do was move as far away from that place as possible. Rachel was right, we should have been more careful.

She followed my glance as we passed the exit for the mountain. "I guess you're right. We need to know more. I just hope Charlie's safe."

CHAPTER NINETEEN_

When I returned home that evening after dropping Rachel off, I messaged Heather like before. Once again, my phone rang in less than a minute, and an odd electronic static pulsated over the line.

"Yes?" a half-robot sounding voice finally said. But it wasn't Heather's sultry Australian tone. Despite the distortion, it was clearly a man.

"Where's Heather?" I asked, thrown by the change.

"Dr. Avanair is not available this evening. What can I help you with, Bryce?"

I recognized him now. It was Sturgis.

"I need to speak with Heath—Dr. Avanair, I mean… or with you… I need to know what happened to Charlie. He's gone missing. I know she said not to worry, but I can't help it. I *am* worried about him."

There was a pause, the buzzing on the line the only sound. "Mr. Kilroy is in good hands. There is nothing for you to worry about," Sturgis replied. "But *I* am worried that you are getting too emotionally involved in things that don't concern you, Bryce. We have things perfectly under control. You only need to focus on the assignments we give you. I won't accept another call like this again. Is that clear?"

I felt my anger rising. I was tired of all this cloak-and-dagger business. They clearly didn't care about any of us.

"Bryce?"

"No, it's not all right," I cried. "I want answers, and I want answers now." I realized I was yelling and tried to get myself back under control. Not so much because I cared about what Sturgis thought, but it was late. Disturbing the rest of the house would only lead to questions I wasn't prepared to answer. "I need to know Charlie's okay," I said more quietly.

"Very well."

"What?"

"Very well," Sturgis repeated. "We'll be waiting for you."

I'd expected more resistance. "Waiting? Where?"

"Here at the lab. You may come tonight if you're so eager for answers. I trust you remember the way."

I tried to process what he was saying. It was already ten o'clock. "You want me to drive up into the mountains tonight? Are you serious?"

Sturgis sighed, his breath broken into odd electronic grumbles and beeps. "I'm not one for joking, Bryce. I'll see you in two hours." And with that, the line went dead.

I leaned back and stared at the phone. What had I just done? Was this an invitation to the truth, or had I just signed my own missing person's report?

I managed to sneak out of the house, rolling the Mustang away from the driveway without drawing attention. All my after-hours programming sessions were making me feel more alert in the middle of the night. The roads were clear as I drove out of Milton and into the mountains. No one else was heading to Tech at that hour, and surely not to where I was going.

I thought about calling Rachel to see if she could join me, but it was no use putting her in danger too. I lingered at the next stop sign and shot her a text.

Driving to lab to meet with Sturgis tonight. If you don't hear from me tomorrow, send help.

At least there would be some record of where I'd been.

The signs for Tech floated silently by, and I wondered if I should turn and track down Dr. Hendrickson or Tyler Barnes instead of meeting with Sturgis. Tyler might live on campus as a graduate student, but neither of them would likely be in the computer lab at this hour. And I had no idea where to start looking for them. No, I'd set this in motion by asking questions. There was no point in stopping now. If they were going to come after me, they'd have done so already like they had with Charlie.

It was dead silent when I pulled up to the Q2 building. Several lights shone across the parking lot, but all the spaces were empty. Maybe Sturgis parked somewhere else. The reception entrance was locked, but a fingerprint scanner was mounted above the latch. Maybe it worked like my laptop. I placed my thumb on the pad, and after a second, the lock clicked open. Bingo.

I walked into the shadowy reception area. No one was at the desk behind the window, of course, so I opened the door beside it and followed the hallway deeper into the building.

My footsteps echoed along the tile. The security lights provided just enough illumination to see but were set at a fraction of their normal capacity. I stopped when the hall split into two directions. What was I even doing here in the middle of the night? I was still a rat in the maze, searching for the cheese.

"Hello, Bryce."

I spun around at the sound of my name, but the hall was empty. I glanced up at a security camera mounted in the corner.

"Turn left. Come to the open door at the end of the hall," the voice boomed again, sounding like the voice of God.

I followed the instructions and stepped into the room behind the open doorway. Rows of tables with computer terminals cast a steady green glow in the otherwise dark room. I wasn't sure why all the monitors would be on in the middle of the night, but nothing made sense right now. Another large wall monitor hung above an instructor's desk.

"Come in," said a man's voice. He stood from behind a workstation in the back of the rom and walked toward me.

Sturgis reached out and shook my hand. "Glad you made it," he said, coolly. "Take a seat."

"It didn't seem like I had much choice," I replied, sitting at the first table.

Sturgis tilted his head like I was talking nonsense. "We always have choices, Bryce. Besides, I believe you called us, did you not? You wanted answers."

I motioned at the room. "You always sit in the dark?"

He ignored me and used a remote to turn on the wall monitor. A stunning picture filled the screen, an aerial view across a glittering row of skyscrapers. The sun reflected off the glass buildings like sparkling crystals. In the foreground sat a wide desk. Then a man walked into view and stood by the desk, the sparkling city behind him through the window.

Yao.

CHAPTER TWENTY_

"Good afternoon, Bryce," Yao said into the camera, an amused expression on his face. "Or should I say, good evening, where you are. Greetings from Shanghai." He waved at the skyline through the wall of glass windows behind him. "The sparkling jewel of the East. Have you ever been to China, Bryce?"

"No."

Yao clucked his disapproval. "Someday perhaps, then." He sat in the chair behind the desk and smiled, like he was in the room with us and not seven thousand miles away on the other side of the world. It felt like his eyes were boring into me.

"Thank you for deciding to pay us another visit," Yao said. "I'm sorry that I can't be with you in person, but business has called me back to the mainland."

"I was summoned," I replied.

"Hmm, well that may be true, but we appreciate your coming nonetheless." He sighed and picked up an ornate pen from his desk, twirling it in his fingers. "I understand that you have some concerns?"

I gulped and thought of the best approach. "Yes, I do. I've been working on the project for a few weeks, but I don't know if I'm the right fit. At least right now with school, and track, and everything at home." I tried to sound convincing. "Maybe in the summer, after I graduate, it might work out better."

Yao nodded. "Of course, that's perfectly understandable."

I relaxed a little. "Thanks. It really is amazing what you're doing here. It's been an honor just being considered. Seriously."

"I agree that for most people, the load would be far too great," Yao said, now scribbling on a pad of paper. "Only the best minds can operate under these kinds of pressures, and I fully acknowledge we've thrown you in the deep end of the pool."

He stopped writing and looked directly at the camera.

At me.

"But then, we both know you are not like most people. Are you, Bryce?"

I didn't know how to answer that. I glanced at Sturgis, standing by the door, but his face was expressionless. "Uh, no, I guess not, but..."

"Of course you're not," said Yao, reassuringly, as if the correct answer had been right in front of us all along. "You and I are alike, Bryce. We're different from everyone else. I've known my entire life that more talent lies in my little finger than in most of the people who walk past me on the street."

He leaned back in his chair. "I was a young man like you once, full of ambition, with dreams to change the world. But contrary to what your Western culture says, not everyone is special. Few individuals truly have an opportunity to be that change. Your friends, Miss Kelly and Mr. Kilroy, are talented programmers to be sure. They have ability, but they're not like you. It was clear to us even before you arrived that you possessed the greatest potential in the entire orientation class. We saw it when we were monitoring your activity in the game. The way you worked through levels, attacked problems, creatively searched for solutions within the *Kingdom* world. Your performance was in the top one percent of everyone we've seen.

"This is your opportunity to get ahead, Bryce. To gain a first-class education with a ready-made career path. And of course, don't forget about the financial burden a fully covered education would lift. I trust that's still important for your family?"

My mouth felt dry. I cleared my throat. "Yes, and that's an amazing offer, but I'm afraid I'm going to have to give that back. I'll just have to find another scholarship, even if it's not as generous." I didn't know what I'd do, but surely I could find something. That had been the plan long before all of this had come along.

Yao clucked his tongue. "I'm afraid it's not quite that simple, Bryce."

I felt warm. The green glow from the computer stations seemed like it was closing in on me. "What do you mean?"

Yao nodded toward the door, and Sturgis stepped forward, holding one of the electronic tablets we'd been given at orientation. "I'm sure you remember the documents you signed when you arrived, Bryce," said Sturgis. "They are fully binding legal contracts, designed to protect us from anyone who gains proprietary knowledge of our operations. You said yourself, this is groundbreaking. We can't let just anyone in."

"The only positions I pay more generously than my

programmers are my lawyers," cackled Yao. "I'm not a man to take chances with contracts. I assure you that what you signed is ironclad."

"In other words, Bryce," said Sturgis. "You cannot undo what you have started here any more than you can go back to the beginning of a race once the starting gun has fired."

What was he saying? It was too late? My hands tightened their grip on the edge of the desk. "But I said I'll give back the scholarship. That's only fair. And I certainly won't tell anyone about what you're working on here. I'll keep quiet, you have my word."

"Of course you will," said Yao, leaning closer to the camera. "But I'm afraid that leaving is still out of the question."

Sturgis held out the tablet as if the facts were obvious. "Not only would leaving forfeit the scholarship associated with this program, but if you had read the fine print of what you signed, you would know that you'd also become ineligible for any other grants or awards. Think of it as trying to reestablish your amateur status with the NCAA after turning pro. It's impossible."

My head was spinning with questions. I thought about running from the room, but I suddenly felt weak. I looked back at the monitor. "What's happened to Charlie?"

Yao waved his hand dismissively. "Mr. Kilroy started down the same road that you are on, but unfortunately he did not make the wise decision. He forced our hands. But that is not of your concern."

I set my jaw. "What happened to him?"

Yao stared back at me. "I like you, Bryce. Do you believe that?"

"Does it matter?"

He chuckled, but then his voice turned colder. "I suppose not. Perhaps you should more fully consider your situation."

"What do you mean?"

Yao flashed a wicked smile. "For example, I'm sure your father wouldn't like to learn that his hot new client could flit away faster than it came?"

I froze. Dad? What did his client have to do with anything? Yao must have been able to read my face.

"Don't be naive, Bryce. Surely you didn't think it was a coincidence that your father suddenly landed a plum new sale, did you? I told you when we first met, I own many businesses, one of which has a division office in Omaha. But their keen interest in the services of your father's company can be taken away very quickly. And I presume his boss wouldn't be pleased to lose such a key account, particularly if your father's performance is blamed. I'd hate to see him back on the job boards again looking for work. Much like you, he seems like a very competent man, but at his age the marketplace can be so...," he paused as if searching for a word, "...unforgiving."

I sat in stunned silence, trying to process what he was saying.

"You see, Bryce, the decisions and commitments that we make have far-reaching impacts. That wasn't as important to someone like Mr. Kilroy, who sadly doesn't have as much to lose, but I think it may prove a strong incentive for a family man like you."

Yao's eyes narrowed. "I'd hate to see anything unfortunate happen to your young brother. And that pretty girlfriend of yours, she might not look kindly on all the time you've been spending with other women, quite beautiful women I might add, like Dr. Avanair or young Rachel. She's understanding, I'm sure, but everyone has their limits. No one likes discovering secrets."

Yao stood and turned to the window, staring out across the city. "But certainly, Bryce, you can leave whenever you'd like. Dr. Sturgis will be happy to show you the door." He turned around and stared at me through the camera. "The decision is yours." Then he pressed a button on his desk, and the video call cut to black.

I slumped back in my chair. My arms felt weighed down, as if I had been handcuffed to the table.

Sturgis opened the door and motioned for me to leave. "We'll assume that you'll be continuing in the program, Bryce. Don't be stupid and make a shortsighted decision that you'll regret later."

I pulled myself up and followed him down the hall. We turned a corner, but Sturgis paused at an unmarked door. He peered through a small window and then glanced back, like he was inviting me to look.

I stepped up to the glass and saw another workroom, like the one we'd just been in. Several people my age were typing at computer stations. But why were they working in the middle of the night?

A boy raised his head and looked at me.

My heart stopped.

It was Charlie.

CHAPTER TWENTY-ONE_

I didn't like to cry. I prided myself on keeping it all together. Being the man in control that everyone could depend on. Sure, I remembered crying when Dad told me Grandpa Jack had died two summers ago, and probably when Mags and I first started dating and we had our first fight, but that was it. Yet as I headed home, tears streamed down my face.

The mountain air was perfectly clear this time, but my head was still lost in a fog. I pulled off the road and into the parking lot at the same scenic overlook I had stopped at on my first trip down the mountain. Lights twinkled for miles down in the valley. It was beautiful, but it all barely registered.

Were the threats from Yao and Sturgis real or just scare tactics? Could Yao actually be connected to Dad's new client, or was he bluffing? There was no way to know. But I hadn't imagined Charlie's face at the computer terminal. The look in his eyes was haunting.

My phone buzzed in my pocket. It was a reply from Tyler. Maybe he hadn't forgotten about me after all. I opened the message and held my breath.

Bryce, I'm very familiar with that topic, but I worry that you may not realize all you're involved with to be asking that question. Call me ASAP. We need to meet.

I'm not sure why I acted so quickly. Maybe I didn't care about the implications, or maybe my mind was just numb. But I didn't think, I just clicked on Tyler's number at the bottom of the message.

"Bryce?" The deep voice spoke without the phone even ringing. It was well past midnight.

"I want to talk," I answered.

"Where are you?"

"Parked at the Bear Claw Overlook."

"Stay there," Tyler instructed. "I'll pick you up in twenty minutes."

Those twenty minutes seemed like hours. The road was still barren. I was the only foolish traveler at two in the morning. I considered hightailing it out of there, but where would I go next? Would I break down and confess everything to my parents? That may have been the right move at the start, but it was impossible now. I was in too deep. Things had progressed too far—there was no turning back. I had to trust someone, and I prayed that Tyler was that person.

I waited in the darkness, sitting on one of the large rocks outlining the parking lot. Any other time, I would have wished I was there stargazing with Maggie, but my mind was too garbled. It immediately sharpened when I heard a noise. I thought it might be Tyler's car, but it wasn't anything mechanical. It was something wild.

The overlook was named Bear Claw. Was that from the

shape of the rock formation or because of its inhabitants? My eyes had adjusted to the moonlight enough that I could see fairly well across the parking lot. A scurrying in the undergrowth didn't sound loud enough to be a bear, but it might be a cub. I'd seen enough National Geographic Channel specials to know that if it was a cub, the mother bear would be close behind, but neither emerged from the bush.

I shined my phone's light in a wide arc around the edges of the pavement. A flash of movement bounced through the beam. Two greenish-yellow circles glowed back at me, eyes reflecting in the light. They stared, unflinching, but then stepped cautiously toward me.

As the animal entered further into the light, I could see the coarse reddish fur. It was a fox. I knew from our annual camping trips not to mess with an animal in the wild. But I couldn't move. I couldn't look away.

Headlights came around the corner quickly. For an instant, the fox was fully illuminated, its entire body visible in the beams. But then it dashed off the blacktop and out of sight. I blinked at the new source of light, breaking free from my trance. A dark-colored SUV pulled into the parking lot next to me. The driver's window lowered.

"Hop in," the man said, seemingly unconcerned that I might be anyone else at this time of night.

I walked around to the other side and climbed into the passenger seat. The man was a few years older than me, but his voice was deep. His dark hair was short, and he was dressed casually in jeans and a T-shirt.

"I'm Tyler. I'm glad you called." He put the SUV in reverse and pulled back onto the road.

"Are you always up this late?" I asked.

Tyler chuckled. "Depends. I guess after enough late nights cramming for exams, you kind of get used to it. Now, I find my head is clearer when everyone else is sleeping."

I thought about all my middle-of-the-night assignments from Heather and nodded.

"What about you?" Tyler asked. "Something tells me you weren't just at the overlook for the late-night view." He paused as we wound around a tight hairpin curve in the road. "You were at Q2, weren't you? To see Sturgis? Or was it the old man himself?"

It felt foreign to be talking to someone about Q2 after so much secrecy. Was he just baiting me, or was he somehow involved? I shifted in my seat uncomfortably, but I realized I was committed now. "How much do you know?"

Tyler bit his bottom lip, his face illuminated by the dashboard's lights. He glanced at me and then back at the road. "I know a lot, Bryce. Believe it or not, I was in your shoes. They recruited me while I was an undergrad at Tech. I was one of the first they approached. This was before they had a full orientation program. Oh, they wined and dined me, filled me with promises of riches and knowledge. They mix in just enough truth to keep you hooked, but there's always a darker side, Bryce. One they never tell you about until it's too late."

"What happened to you?" I asked.

Tyler let out a long breath. "I got out, but I was lucky. They hadn't yet tightened all their contracts and legal processes, and I was fortunate to have a good relationship with one of my professors, Dr. Hendrickson. Early on, I made the smart choice to tell him everything, and he helped me escape."

I thought back to the curious encounter I'd had with Dr.

Hendrickson on the student tour at Tech. How he'd asked me to work on equations in the lab. "What did he do?"

Tyler hesitated, as if trying to decide how much to share with a kid he'd just picked up in the middle of nowhere. But I also had the sense that he knew much more about me than I did of him. "I found out there was a lot more to my professor than I'd realized."

Now he was talking like Yao and Sturgis. I was tired of speaking in codes. "More what?"

"I think it will be easier if I show you," replied Tyler. "We'll be there soon."

Alarms went off in my head. Where was he taking me? I hadn't been paying attention to where he was driving, but now I searched for landmarks. "I thought we were going to Tech?"

"It's close by, and I promise, you'll be perfectly safe. You have my word," Tyler said calmly.

I didn't know what to say, so we rode silently until Tyler pulled onto an unmarked trail that reminded me of Charlie's road. It was so narrow that the trees smacked at the side mirrors. We wound along over the bumpy road for a minute or two until we reached a dead end. I prayed this wasn't where he killed me or where Yao and Sturgis stepped out of the woods in ambush.

Tyler lowered his window and typed something into a hidden keypad. A camouflaged gate slowly rolled back, allowing us to pass before returning into place. We continued to a second security gate, this one clearly visible and manned by an armed guard. He looked like he was military as he stepped out to check Tyler's credentials. He shined a light across the seat into my face, but Tyler assured him I was okay.

We pulled forward into a parking lot before a darkened

building. It felt like I was arriving back at Q2 all over again. I turned and looked at Tyler hesitantly.

"Come on," he said, opening his door. "It will all make sense soon."

CHAPTER TWENTY-TWO_

Entering the building had seemed like something from a Bond movie—guard booths, rooms with secret elevators in the floor.

"Is this a cave?" I asked, peering around the enormous room we'd entered.

"Close to it," answered Tyler. "Where we're standing used to be an old military compound that was built into an underground cavern. It already had security measures constructed, which makes it the perfect place for our work."

"And what exactly is it you do here?" I blinked as a series of round LEDs, like the ones in our school gym, slowly came to life. Several banks of computer stations lined the walls, but what really caught my attention was the large object in the center of the room that looked a little like… a spaceship.

I had an odd sense of déjà vu. The room differed completely from the large programming lab at Q2, and the object didn't look much like the Eden Machine, but my brain told me it was related.

Tyler seemed to read my thoughts. "What do you think?"

I yawned and walked toward the object. "I think I've been awake too long." I placed my hand on the metal. It had the same smooth silver finish as Eden, but it was cool to the touch. Maybe it was from the overall temperature of the cavern, which seemed a good ten degrees colder than outside. "Is this what I think it is?"

Tyler grinned, but didn't answer. He turned on several computers, and streams of code poured across a screen in front of the machine. It was too fast to read, but I could tell they were sophisticated sequences. A few more keystrokes slowed the stream to a readable level.

I saw it immediately. It was the same type of programming as I'd been working on in my assignments. How was that possible?

A new concern flooded my mind. I stepped back. Maybe this was all part of an elaborate trap. Was Yao testing me to see if I'd talk?

I turned to Tyler. "Where did you get this? Are you part of Q2?"

He held up his hand reassuringly. "We're not Q2, I promise. But we're working on similar initiatives. Fitz was one of Dr. Hendrickson's early partners, but he left our program and forged an alliance with Yao and Sturgis. Together they built Q2 on the other side of the mountain."

I shivered remembering the creepy, giant man who ran the main lab back at Q2's compound.

"Dr. Hendrickson and Tech's *Advanced Digital Sciences Division* are working in concert with the U.S. government to develop technology to beat Q2 across the digital bridge. We call our initiative Project JOSHUA."

"Joshua?" I asked, remembering how the voice in the vent had used that phrase.

"*Journeys Outside Standard Human Understanding and Advancement*," Tyler explained. "It's largely Hendrickson's brainchild, but there's a large team working on it. And yes, the machine and the coding looks familiar to you because it follows a similar concept pattern to the Eden project."

They'd talked in orientation about working to get ahead of the competition, but I never dreamed that the competition was the United States government. Did that make me a traitor?

"Ji Yao is not a nice man, Bryce. His goal is nothing short of world domination, with the Chinese as the preeminent global power. Any organization, be it a country or a tech company like Q2, that develops the ability to bridge the digital frontier will be immensely powerful—and extremely dangerous."

"But you're trying to do the same thing," I said. "Isn't that just as dangerous?"

Tyler tilted his head. "Sometimes the most important reason to have advanced technology is to block the wrong people from using it. Think about nuclear weapons."

"Didn't the United States bomb Japan?"

"Yes, but think about the Cold War."

"The Russians had nukes, too. It wasn't just America." There seemed to be a lot of holes in his analogy.

"But they never used them. Why not?"

"Because they knew that if they did, we'd retaliate with ours."

Tyler nodded. "Exactly. It was a mutual deterrence."

I tried to determine if he was making sense, but my brain

moved slowly. “So, you’re not going to use this JOSHUA machine if you get it working? You won’t try to cross the digital bridge?”

“I don’t know what we’ll do, but allowing Yao and Q2 to exclusively wield such power would put the world in much greater peril.” He placed a hand on my shoulder. “Sometimes we’re put in a position for a reason. You can make a difference here, Bryce.”

I shook my head and pulled away. “Yao fed me that same line.” I recounted to Tyler Q2’s legal traps, their threats to ruin Dad’s business, and even hurt Maggie and Zach. “I can’t let anything happen to them.”

“I understand,” said Tyler. “But don’t you see? Helping us is the only way to stop them.”

I rubbed my forehead. Not only should I have been in bed hours ago, but Tyler wasn’t listening. “I just told you; I can’t help you. They won’t let me.”

“I understand it’s difficult, but that doesn’t mean it’s impossible.”

I looked up at him. “Then how?”

“Bryce, the facts are that we’ve fallen behind Q2. They’ve achieved great success using *Final Kingdom* to pull in bright minds like yours. It’s given them the advantage they needed to turbocharge their efforts. They’ve leapfrogged us over the past twelve months, and we believe they are dangerously close to completing a bridge.”

I thought back to everything that Charlie, Rachel, and I had been working on. While we only had parts of the overall puzzle, it seemed like the pieces were fitting together, and Yao had made his intentions perfectly clear.

“We need copies of their research and their coding

sequences so we can catch back up. If we can build the bridge first, then we can block their efforts. We cannot allow Yao and the Chinese to have this technology. There's too much at stake."

I took a deep breath. "So you want me to sabotage their systems? I don't think they'd let me close enough to do that."

"Perhaps eventually," said Tyler. "But right now, we just need copies of your programming. This will help." He held up a slim, electronic device that looked similar to a mini external hard drive that could fit into a standard computer port.

"What's that, a bomb?"

Tyler shook his head. "More like a digital scanner. It has software that seamlessly mirrors your programming interface. It's completely invisible to Q2, but it will securely transmit copies of your work back to us."

I took the device and turned it over in my hand. "Sounds risky. What if they catch me?"

"They won't."

"Easy for you to say. You'll be safe on the receiving end, but they'll be coming after me. What do I do then?" I told him how I'd seen Charlie earlier that night working in Q2's lab.

Tyler pursed his lips seriously. "What other choice do you have, Bryce? It sounds like you've exhausted your options. Isn't this why you contacted me?"

"I could just keep doing what they tell me. Your project isn't my problem."

"And then what, Bryce? Become a slave to Ji Yao and the Chinese? This isn't just about you now. This is about helping your country. Your world. How many other kids like Charlie are you going to let go missing? It must be stopped."

I thought back to my first night in the Q2 compound. The guy through the vent had told me to find Tyler. What happened to him after they dragged him from his room? Was he slaving away like Charlie in a secured computer lab writing code for Yao? Was he dead? Was there a difference?

I stared at the mirroring device in my hand. The harsh reality of my situation was obvious. Maybe it had been all along, and I just hadn't wanted to see it. There was no choice at all, really. I had to do what Tyler asked. I had to leak the code.

There was no other way.

CHAPTER TWENTY-THREE_

Dawn was still an hour or two away when Tyler dropped me back at the overlook's parking lot.

"Hold up," he said, then pulled an electronic device from the back seat of his SUV. It was mounted on a thin rod, making it look like a metal detector. But instead of running the device along the pavement, he held it under the undercarriage of the Mustang and circled the car. "We can't be too careful."

It started beeping quickly as he neared the trunk. He dropped onto his back, sliding under the rear bumper. A few seconds later, he emerged holding up a black object the size of a matchbox car. "Looks like you're being tracked."

"By Q2?"

Tyler nodded. "Unless your girlfriend is more possessive than most."

Panic shot through me. I stared up the dark road, lowering my voice to a whisper. "Then they know I'm here? That we're meeting?"

"No, it's not a recorder. They can't hear us. It feeds into a

GPS system to track your location." He removed the plastic cover, pulled out a small battery, and then stomped on the tracker with his shoe. "That should keep them off you for a while. If they question why you stopped here for so long, just say you got tired and snoozed for a couple hours."

"What about the tracker?"

"They'll likely assume it just fell off. It happens."

Tyler seemed to have an answer for everything. Was he a computer programmer or a super spy? Maybe he was a little of both. He went over the instructions for using the mirroring device on my laptop one more time, and then we parted ways.

As I drove down the mountain, I began to craft an explanation for Mom, Dad, or Zach if they caught me coming in at the break of dawn. The lies were flowing pretty naturally now. I didn't like that, but I rationalized that I had no choice. Thankfully, it was Saturday, and I didn't have to go to school or track practice. I was supposed to work at the store, but I called in sick, leaving a message saying I had been up all night puking. Then I shot Rachel a text that I was back home and safe.

I rolled to a stop in front of my house, closing the car door silently, and crept into the garage, hoping to make it to my room without being seen.

"You're out early this morning."

Dad's voice nearly sent me out of my shoes. "Oh, hey, Dad. I didn't see you there." I quickly shifted to my backup plan and tried to act normal. "Yeah, I was supposed to meet up with Tony this morning for a run, but he overslept, so I came home."

Dad glanced at my clothes, which weren't my normal running attire.

"I brought a gym bag in the car," I explained, and then I tried to change the subject. "What are you doing out here?" He was carrying his toolbox, and sweat and grease streaked his shirt.

"AC unit's not running." He wiped a dirty hand across his forehead. "Didn't you notice it last night?"

"Oh, yeah," I said. "It was hot." The air in the mountains had been cool thanks to the higher elevation, but down here in the valley, the air was already thick, even in the early morning.

"Give your old man a break and carry these." Dad handed me the heavy metal toolbox, and I followed him around the side of the house. The grass was turning brown from lack of rain. We stopped at the compressor unit.

"Is it broken?" I asked.

"Might be."

"You know how to fix it?"

Dad sighed. "Not really. Ed Janakowski walked by a few minutes ago with his dog. He was looking at it with me, but between us, I don't think he really knows what he's talking about either."

"So you're back where you started?"

"Yup. Probably gonna have to get the service company out here to look at it." He sat gently on the toolbox and wiped his brow. "Of course, this heat wave will probably be over by the time I get on their schedule."

I felt hot just talking about it. "That sucks."

"Yeah," moaned Dad. "But at least it won't be expensive."

"No?"

He patted my shoulder. "I'm kidding, son. Everything's expensive."

I was struggling to keep my eyes open. "Anything I can do?"

"Why don't you get a couple fans down from the attic and place them in the bedrooms? We're going to need them if we want to sleep any better tonight."

"Sure thing, Dad."

Zach came around the corner holding a glass.

"Hey," I said. "What's that?"

"Lemonade. Mom said that Dad could probably use it."

Dad downed the drink in one long gulp and handed back the glass. "Thanks, son."

"I'll go get those fans," I said.

"Where you been?" Zach asked, following me to the front porch. "Aren't you supposed to be at work?"

I fibbed that I had taken today off from the store and repeated the story of my failed attempt to run with Tony. Zach eyed me expectantly. I knew he probably wanted to hang out. We'd fallen out of our normal routine of playing *Kingdom* together on the weekends since I had started working Saturdays at the store. Now with all the craziness, it was even worse.

"Let's hang out this afternoon, okay?" I felt bad, but I desperately needed to lie down.

"Whatever," he said, but his frown showed his true feelings. "Andrew's coming over after lunch."

"Tomorrow then?"

"Sure. If you even remember how to play."

Another wave of guilt swept through me. "Don't worry, I think about it more than you'd guess."

I managed to get a couple hours sleep before lunch with no one bothering me, but it wasn't enough, and I headed to bed earlier than usual that night. My bedroom windows were open since the AC was down, but even with the air circulating thanks to the fan I'd found in the attic, it was still hot.

I was about to climb into bed, my body already winding down for a solid block of rest, when the message came. I cursed and nearly threw the laptop out the open window as I read Heather's instructions for more programming sequences due in the morning. I rubbed my face and then picked up Tyler's mirroring device. Was it worth the risk? What if it wasn't invisible like he'd claimed and it sets off alarm bells at Q2 the moment I plugged it into the silver laptop? Would they come and take me away like they had Charlie?

I couldn't shake Tyler's words from my memory. What was the alternative? Endless middle-of-the-night requests like this one only to advance Yao's evil plans? No, I couldn't be part of that.

The device immediately glowed blue when I fit it into a drive port and opened the programming interface. I took a deep breath and began my work. With each blue pulse from the device, I was moving closer to helping Tyler and Hendrickson's JOSHUA project succeed, or to my own demise.

I was making good progress on the assignment. I'd heard the rest of my family head off to bed, and the house fell quiet aside from my constant typing and the rhythmic whir of the fan. The sound of the night filled my room, playing in its own rhythm and moving along as usual, despite the deep hole I'd stumbled into. The street had been quiet since Mr. Harper had passed with Sadie a while back, taking her on her usual walk before bed. So when a car passed, I took notice, glancing up as the taillights drifted past slowly, then fell out of sight. I sank back into my work, but a minute later, the sound of an engine again caught my ear.

Every motor has a unique sound if you listen carefully enough. Even those new electric cars that sneak up on you probably have their own hum. My Mustang's engine had seen better days, but I found its gentle rumble comforting as I drove around town. So when the car pulled onto our street, I recognized the engine as the same one that had passed by before. Was it circling the block?

The motor slowed and then seemed to idle outside our house. I dimmed the light at my desk, moving to the window and peering at the street from behind my curtain. A vehicle sat motionless on the far curb. Its lights were dimmed, but the engine was still running. A faint shadow of the driver was visible from the dashboard's glow. What were they doing?

I glanced over my shoulder at the blinking blue light in the laptop. Had Q2 detected the mirroring device? Were they watching me from the street right now? I looked at the clock and rubbed my eyes. After midnight again. Maybe I was just getting overly tired and a bit paranoid. It could be anybody out there.

But then I heard the car door open. Footsteps walked along the pavement. I squinted through the dark. A figure stood at the end of the driveway. A metal creaking came from the rusty hinge of our mailbox that Dad kept forgetting to oil.

A rush of adrenaline and frustration filled me. I silently raised the window screen and climbed into the flowerbed. Having a single-story ranch home had its advantages for sneaking out, although I'd rarely done so over the years. I crouched low and watched for movement. The shadow returned to the car. The door shut. They were getting away!

I jumped up and bolted toward the road, leaping over the bushes next to the curb and landing gracefully on the pavement in my bare feet. The car engine revved as it pulled out. I sprinted behind it until the next block, but it got further and further away. There was no chance I would catch it. It turned onto Atlantic and sped out of sight.

I stopped in the middle of the road and bent over at the waist to catch my breath. The neighborhood was silent. I was the only fool out chasing cars in the middle of the night. I turned and walked gingerly back to our mailbox, my feet sore from the pavement. I eyed the metal box hesitantly. The figure had put something in it. A bomb, set to explode as soon as I opened the door? Maybe they'd wired it to the flag.

I rubbed my eyes again. It was too late. If this was the end, I might as well get it over with. I held my breath and creaked open the metal door. No explosion. I peered inside. I didn't see any wires or sticks of dynamite, just a lone manila envelope, stuffed in the box at an angle. Why would someone put an envelope in our mailbox in the middle of the night? I slid the envelope out and carried it back to my window.

The envelope's metal clasp opened easily, and glossy sheets of paper slipped out. I picked several index-card-sized papers off the desk. Photographs. Of me and Rachel—in the lab at orientation, in my car, outside Charlie's house. Someone was following us. Watching us. Maybe they were watching me right now. Was this the only set that had been delivered? Had someone also dropped some in Maggie's mailbox?

I looked down at the mirroring device and shook my head. Tyler had assured me it was safe, untraceable. But we'd already found a tracker on my car. Now these pictures. How could I be sure he knew what he was talking about? Who could I trust?

Regardless of their ultimate intentions, I feared that Q2 and Tyler had one thing in common—both cared more about advancing their causes than my safety. Rachel, Charlie, and I were just pawns. Pieces to be used for their end game. Valuable because of what we could do for them, but ultimately as expendable as an avatar within *Kingdom*. But a *GAME OVER* message here in the real world would have a far more lasting impact for me than it did online.

I needed to call Rachel again. We had to gain some leverage, find some insurance, in case anything happened to us. They'd already come for Charlie. It could only be a matter of time until we were next.

CHAPTER TWENTY-FOUR_

Three more assignments came in over the next couple weeks. Pulling the late-night jobs still wasn't easy, but Tyler had been right about one thing, I was getting used to it. Even with the tight deadline pressure, coding through the night had its own rhythm. It was driven by a peaceful silence, knowing that everyone else was asleep.

Despite my anxiety, I continued to connect the mirroring device. The pictures in the mailbox were a warning, meant to scare me, but now I was in too deep. In addition to my work for Q2, Tyler had begun sending assignments to my personal laptop. I figured that the more I helped complete gaps in his code, the faster JOSHUA could catch up with Eden. I'd called Rachel the morning after they left the photographs and told her about my meeting with Tyler. She'd agreed to help too, and soon she was sending Tyler her own Q2 coding through a secure online drop. It wasn't as quick and seamless as the mirroring device on my laptop, but it seemed to work. Tyler assured us we were helping, that we were serving our country, and that it would all be over soon.

I almost believed him. I knew it would be over soon, but I was unsure who would go down in flames—Yao and Q2, or Rachel and me. I regularly had nightmares now, vivid dreams of being chased by shadowy figures that watched my every move. Sometimes I saw Charlie's face in the lab, other times Ji Yao came over for dinner and exposed all my lies to Maggie and my disappointed family. It was like all the secrets were overloading my brain and popping out in my subconscious. With each passing day, I started to feel less like myself inside. It was as if the real me was slowly slipping away, like grains of sand on the shoreline, beaten and pulled back by the tides bit by bit.

After I finished working at the store on a Saturday, Dad asked me to pick up an extra box of air filters for the new AC unit that had finally been installed. The hardware store was across the shopping center from where I worked, so I left the Mustang parked and walked along the covered sidewalk. I stopped and glanced at the window display in the gift and card store between the nail salon and pizza place. It was nearly the anniversary of my first date with Maggie. I needed a gift, and a placard next to some jewelry caught my eye.

Free personalized engraving with purchase.

I walked in and browsed the front display cases. I wasn't after anything too fancy—most of it was above my budget anyway—but I knew she'd appreciate something simple and pretty. My eye settled on a silver pendant and chain. I leaned closer to inspect it.

"That's a beautiful piece." A saleswoman hovered on the other side of the case. "It makes a perfect gift for that special someone. Would you like to see it?"

I glanced up and nodded. "Sure." I'd never really bought jewelry before, but it seemed nice.

She unlocked the glass case and pulled out the thin box. She lifted the pendant and handed it to me, the chain coiling softly in my palm. I held the silver charm with my fingers. Its shape was abstract, a cross between a heart and a shark's tooth.

"We offer free engraving, if you're interested," said the woman.

I turned the pendant over and watched it catch the light. "It's not too small for that?"

"Not at all. It can fit a short phrase like 'I love you,' a word from a poem, or a scripture reference, perhaps? Anything not too lengthy."

I glanced at the price tag. It was a little over two hundred dollars.

"And," said the saleswoman, smelling a potential sale, "today we're running a twenty-percent-off sale for first-time customers."

I figured that was just a line to get me to buy it, but it worked. "I'll take it."

She flashed a twinkly smile. "Wonderful. And would you like it engraved?"

"How long does that take?"

"Oh, just a couple days. But if you need it sooner, we can probably accommodate you." She took the necklace and placed it back in the box. "What do you think?"

I formed a plan in my mind. "I'll pay for it now, but can I call you later with the inscription?"

"I don't see why not. Need to search your heart for just the right message?"

"Something like that."

"How sweet. She's a lucky girl to have such a thoughtful boyfriend."

I nodded uneasily. If she only knew.

* * *

WATER SPLASHED from potholes filled by rain from the storm the night before as we pulled down the quiet path just before dark.

"Where are you taking me?" Maggie giggled nervously, leaning forward to look at the trees that surrounded us. "This is like where they find bodies buried. I have to be back for my field trip to the art museum tomorrow, you know."

I gave her my best psycho-killer stare. "There's something I've been meaning to tell you…" I reached across the seat and placed one hand playfully around her throat.

She laughed and pushed my arm away. "You're crazy."

"A little. For you."

"Seriously, where are you taking me? This has nothing to do with a certain anniversary date coming up, does it?" She reached over and ran her fingers through my hair.

I tried to look confused. "Anniversary? Sorry, I don't know what you're talking about."

Mags shook her head. "Yeah, yeah."

We pulled up to the base of the water tower, and I shut off the engine.

"What is *that*?" Maggie exclaimed, pointing at the dark shadow looming overhead.

"You've never been back here?"

She shook her head and eyed me suspiciously. "Have you? And if so, with *whom*?"

"Uh…" I quickly hopped out of the car. "Never mind. Come on."

Maggie followed me to the base of the water tower, but backed up when I put a foot on the bottom rung of the ladder.

"You gotta be kidding," she said. "I'm not going up there."

"It's fine. I tested it yesterday."

"Sure you did. What's her name?"

I grinned, but decided that any joke I made would probably lead to trouble, or a truth I didn't want to disclose. "It was just me," I lied, taking her hand and leading her back to the ladder. "Come on."

If I hadn't already been up there with Charlie, I'd never have considered taking Maggie. But the steps were wide and secure, with a small guardrail along the sides. Plus, the view from the top was unbeatable.

I turned and stared into her eyes. "Trust me."

She reluctantly nodded and followed behind. As we ascended the tower, I felt the jewelry box in my back pocket. "You okay?" I called back, hoping she was too preoccupied with the height to stare at my butt and notice the box.

"Never better."

I suppose that some girls wouldn't have followed me up there, but I loved Mags' adventurous streak. Rarely had we come across a challenge that she wouldn't try. I pushed away questions about whether I deserved her unwavering trust, given all the secrets I was keeping.

"Almost there."

I reached the platform and extended my arm to help pull her next to me under the water tank. She stepped up, clutching the railing tightly while she got her bearings.

"What do you think?" I waved toward the tops of the

highest pines. The view was better in the fading light than it had been in the full darkness with Charlie. It felt like we were masters of the forest, living in our own personal tree house.

"Oh, wow." She stared across the valley. "Is that the school over there? You can see almost all of Milton. It's beautiful."

"So are you," I said, wrapping her in my arms. I pulled the jewelry box from my pocket. "Happy anniversary."

She turned toward me and smiled. "Was this all part of an elaborate plan to get me alone?"

"Maybe."

"I don't think my mom would approve of my being up in a place like this, with a guy like you."

"Please. You know she loves me." I pointed at the box. "Aren't you going to open it?"

"If it's a bungee cord, I'm not jumping."

I laughed. "Box is too small. But a good idea for next time."

She tugged on the thin red ribbon, catching her breath as she opened the lid and lifted the pendant.

"It's a promise chain," I explained. "A promise that we're committed to each other, no matter what happens."

"It's gorgeous, Bryce." She reached up and kissed me. "Thank you." Then she pulled the hair off her neck and leaned forward. "Help me put it on."

I secured the clasp behind her neck, careful not to drop it over the side. She held the pendant in her fingers, catching the fading light in the silver. As she turned it over, she saw the writing. "Oh, it's engraved?" She moved it closer to read. "What's it say?"

I chuckled nervously, realizing the explanation would sound weird.

I'd decided that I needed insurance, some protection in case anything happened to me. So I'd begun hiding portions of code from both Q2 and Tyler. I stored the additional sequences in a secret execute file accessible only through the password I'd had engraved on the back of Maggie's pendant.

X2T924H24JSK.

No matter what happened to me, she'd keep it safe, and to anyone else, it would be a meaningless sequence of random letters and numbers. I hoped it gave me something that both sides needed, something to keep me in the mix, perhaps even keep me alive.

"It's a code," I answered.

"A code? Like a programmer's?"

I shook my head. "More like a passcode."

"To what?"

"Well, it's supposed to be a passcode to my heart. You've cracked it." It sounded even worse than it had in my head. "Sorry, it seemed romantic at the store."

Maggie thought about it for a moment. "No, that's sweet. Thank you. I love it." She flashed me a sly smile. "Now if only I'd brought a present for you." She wrapped her arms around my neck. "I love you, Bryce. I knew it from the very beginning."

"You did?"

The evening light sparked in her eyes. "Oh, yeah."

I squeezed her tight. "I love you too. You mean so much to me. I hope you'll always remember that."

"Remember?" She stared back at me. "I'm not going anywhere. Are you?"

I closed my eyes and pulled her closer, burying my secret worries deep inside. "Of course not."

We sat together for a long time, my arm around her shoulder and our feet dangling over the platform edge. The sun sank into the horizon, and the sky exploded in a tapestry of vibrant orange and red. As I held her there, secure in my arms, I swore I wouldn't let anything happen to her or any of the people I loved, despite whatever foolish choices I'd made.

I think a lot about that night.

If I had known that it would be the last time we were together, I may never have climbed down from that tower.

CHAPTER TWENTY-FIVE_

I nearly stopped to pick Maggie up for school the next morning, but halfway up her street I remembered she'd gone in early for her class trip to the art museum. When my cell rang at lunch, I assumed it was her, but I looked and saw it wasn't her number. I walked to the picnic tables outside the cafeteria to answer it.

"Rachel?"

"Bryce, hi."

"What's up? Are you okay?"

"I think so, sorry to bother you. I just felt like I needed to check in. I've been so tied up at night with assignments. Has anything changed on your end?"

"No, but I think we're going to make it," I replied, glancing behind me to make sure no one was listening. "Tyler's last message said we'd filled in large gaps for them. They're still trying to fix some problem with energy levels, but he thinks they're close. The only worry is that Q2 might finish first."

I hadn't told Rachel about the necklace password or the code I was securing away in the hidden files. I wasn't sure why.

It seemed like the less people who knew about it, the better my leverage.

"Still no word from Charlie?"

"I don't think he's coming back, Rachel. I told you I saw him in the lab. He wasn't there by choice."

The line was silent.

My dreams about Charlie were coming more often now. I'd see him staring at me from across the room with vacant zombie eyes. It was terrible.

The bell rang for the end of the period, and students began moving past me to head to their next class. "Rachel, I'm sorry. I've gotta go. I'll let you know if I hear anything."

"Okay, thanks. Bye."

The forecast called for thunderstorms all afternoon. So, in a rare act of kindness, Coach Simmons canceled practice. Maggie was having dinner with two of her girlfriends after the trip to the museum, so I drove straight home.

A repair truck was in our driveway when I pulled up to the house. Our new AC compressor had been installed a couple weeks earlier, and Dad had been right, it was expensive—over a thousand dollars. Dad still thought it wasn't cooling properly, and repairmen had already been to the house at least twice to fiddle with it. Normally Dad wouldn't have them come until he was home from work, but he was away overnight in Omaha for a meeting. He must have wanted it fixed before he returned.

I parked in the street so that van would be able to leave. As I reached the front porch, I noticed the repairman was still in the driver's seat. He opened his door and waved me over.

"Is this the Pearson house? 56 Morehead Road?"

You'd think they'd know us by now. "Yep," I answered,

walking over to him. "Are you looking at the compressor? Did my dad call you?"

The man tapped on his routing tablet and nodded. "Right. Something about it still not cooling in all the bedrooms?" He stepped out of the van and hitched up his pants. "We would have been here this morning, but we've been slammed with all this hot weather. Can you point me toward the compressor unit?"

"Yeah, it's over here." I moved to cross in front of the van to show him where Dad had been working.

A blur of motion shot out from beside the van. Two beefy hands grabbed me by the shoulders. They pushed a strip of duct tape over my mouth just before a dark sack came down over my head. I tried to break free, but whoever was holding me was strong.

"Did you find it?" asked the driver.

"Piece of cake," a second man answered, his voice deep and gravelly. "The tracker worked nicely. He had it behind a drawer in his bed. Not very difficult."

They'd gone for the laptop. Of course.

"Found something else too," said the deep voice.

I closed my eyes inside the dark hood. I didn't need to see to know what he was holding up. I'd foolishly left the monitoring device attached to the laptop. There would be no doubt about my actions now. It had only been a matter of time until they came for me, and I'd handed them damning proof.

The van door slid open. I kicked my legs, twisting wildly, as they tried to pick me up. An image of Charlie flashed through my mind.

Then everything went black.

* * *

My face ached. I opened my eyes, but it was so dark I still couldn't see. I tried to move, but they had secured my arms and legs with restraints. I tried to scream, but my mouth was still sealed shut.

I was in a moving vehicle. The van. I remembered the repairman in the driveway. They'd grabbed me, just like they'd grabbed Charlie.

Had anyone seen them take me? The chances were slim. No one would have looked twice at a repair van in our driveway. Business as usual.

Each time the van drove over a bump, my head banged against the metal floor. My restraints were connected to the van. I couldn't see, and it was pointless to move or try to speak. My ear was pressed against the floor, but I didn't even attempt to pinpoint any distinguishing sounds. I already knew where they were taking me. The only question that remained was would they torture me, or just make me work in the lab? Either way, eventually someone would find my lifeless body dumped along the side of a mountain road, if the bears and vultures didn't discover it first.

The van finally pulled to a stop after what felt like days. My hands and feet were numb, and my hip ached from lying on the metal floor at an odd angle. My face felt like it had just gone ten rounds with Mike Tyson thanks to the regular banging against the floorboards. The van doors slid open, and they carried me inside.

When the black hood was finally removed, I was in a room much like the one I'd slept in during orientation. The van driver and a second man with huge hands cut the plastic restraints from my feet and arms. The driver eyed me seriously, as if to make it clear that I shouldn't scream before he ripped off the tape in a fast pull. It hurt like hell, but somehow I managed to stay silent. They attached a hard plastic band to my right ankle that flashed every few seconds. I figured it was a tracking device to prevent me from running. Once they seemed satisfied that the band was functioning properly, both men left the room. The door locked behind them.

I stretched, gradually working the blood back into my arms and legs, and then made a long-delayed trip to the bathroom. A plate of food and a glass of water had been placed on the small table next to the bed. I sat and ate the food—just a simple piece of chicken, some peas, and rice—and washed it down with the water. I stretched out in the bed, staring at the blinking red light on the sprinkler. I touched the tracker on my ankle, but it was secured too tight for me to even scratch an itch.

There was nothing left to do. My body felt squeezed and wrung out like a towel. There was no way to know how long I'd be kept there. It was early, but I was exhausted, and soon I fell asleep.

CHAPTER TWENTY-SIX_

I woke with a start. Faint light streamed through the windows at the ceiling. The electronic lock beeped from the door. Was this how it would be? Cell doors unlocking to start each day? My food dishes were gone from the table, replaced by a simple set of folded clothes—khakis, pale blue T-shirt, thin white hoodie, socks, and underwear—sitting next to my sneakers and a basic toiletries set.

It was unnerving to know that someone had come into my room while I was sleeping. Had it been the goons from the van? Heather? Sturgis? I rubbed my eyes and walked to the shower.

It didn't matter. Nothing did now.

I was trapped.

I stayed in the shower a long time, letting the hot water stream over my body. As terrible as I'd felt back home, this was worse. They had taken me from my family without warning. Now I was hidden away in this place that no one knew existed. What had my parents and Zach thought when they'd returned home from work and school to find me gone? How long would it take for them to call the police? Had they spoken to Maggie? Did they check the store? I thought about how worried they must be, about giving Mags the pendant up on the water tower. Would that be the last time I ever held her?

An unfamiliar guard was waiting outside my room after I'd dressed and stepped into the hall. I followed him into the elevator and down to the second floor without complaint. He escorted me to a small computer lab, much like the one where I'd met Sturgis for our late-night video call to China. It might have even been the same room, although it was hard to tell. They all looked alike.

A table of breakfast food was set up along the wall—bagels, fruit, muffins, coffee, and orange juice. If I had been at a hotel, it would have been a nice continental breakfast, but my present circumstances made it less appealing. My stomach growled and I filled a plate anyway. Staging a hunger strike probably wouldn't help anything.

I nearly choked on my food when the door opened and I saw who walked through. My spoon dropped from my hand and clanged on the floor as Rachel and Charlie entered the room. I leapt up to greet them. Rachel ran over and wrapped me in a hug, choking back sobs.

I pulled back and looked at them both. "Are you all right?"

Charlie was stone-faced, but Rachel nodded through her tears. "Yes. They didn't hurt me. I'm just scared."

"Me too," I said. "Charlie?"

He gave me an emotionless handshake. "Good to see you, brother." He looked different from when I'd seen him at the water tower. His eyes weren't red. In fact, he seemed extraordinarily calm.

"Are you okay?" I asked, wondering if they had drugged or sedated him. He nodded, but all he said was, "Sure."

"Are you hungry?" I pointed to the food table.

"Starving, actually," said Rachel.

They both filled their plates and sat around my table. I described my abduction to Rachel and learned that she'd been taken in much the same way.

"We drove to your house," I told Charlie, as he silently ate his food. "We met your grandma, I think, but you'd already gone."

"Did the men posing as electronics people take you?" asked Rachel.

Charlie nodded. "Yeah. I tried to fight them, but I think they tased me."

"Ouch," said Rachel. "I'm so sorry."

"I saw you in the lab that night when I came to speak to Sturgis," I said, hoping to pull him from his trance.

Rachel touched his arm. "Are you still coding sequences for Eden?"

Charlie nodded between bites of fruit. "I've been helping Fitz aggregate your work. The bridge is nearly done. He thinks it should be operational within the month."

He spoke matter-of-factly, as if he were sharing the weather forecast. There was no hint in his voice that the world could be in imminent peril. Maybe he didn't know. But I suspected that all of us knew, deep down.

"Whatever bee you put in their bonnet," he said, "they hate you more now than they hate me, and I didn't think that was possible."

Rachel glanced at me, her face a mix of frustration and despair. "What are we going to do?"

"I don't know," I whispered, just as the door opened and Sturgis and Heather entered the room.

"Good morning," said Sturgis, smiling like nothing was wrong. Like he was delivering his welcome speech from orientation. "I'm glad you got something to eat. It's good to have you all back."

Heather was silent and avoided eye contact with me as she switched on the large wall monitor. I wondered if she'd signed on for kidnapping teenagers, or if they had coerced her like the rest of us. A familiar dark desk filled the screen, backdropped by a million sparkling lights of the darkened Shanghai skyline.

We waited in silence until Yao moved into the frame, sitting gently at the desk. He busied himself with papers for a few seconds, as if to show that he was a very busy man, then he folded his hands and stared up at the camera, granting us his full attention. He wore no fake smiles this time, his expression stern.

"I had hoped to avoid this conversation, but I see that you could not follow instructions. You have not honored the commitment that each of you made during orientation." He paused, as if considering his next words carefully. "I realize you do not value that word in your Western culture, but *honor* is very important to me. In China, as in much of the East, it is everything."

"Kidnapping three teenagers doesn't seem very honorable," said Rachel, tears again streaming down her face.

"They'll come looking for us," I said. "They'll call the police."

"Police?" Yao clucked his tongue. "Think of this as early enrollment into the work program that you voluntarily agreed to undertake. Each of you had such promise and every opportunity to do things the easy way. Now…," he paused, narrowing his eyes, "the path will be less easy—although just as productive. Perhaps even more so, for me at least. But I'm afraid that your other opportunities for advancement, scholarships, and benefits to your parents' businesses have vanished."

"You won't get away with this," I growled.

"Oh, but I already have, Bryce. You may be special, but you're not irreplaceable. Our mission will continue despite your foolish efforts to the contrary. You cannot stand in the way of progress. Once the Eden project is completed, the land of the Red Dragon will be awakened, and China will take its rightful place of honor as the preeminent world power."

Yao stood and nodded at the camera. "Now I'm afraid I have other pressing commitments, but I will leave you in very competent hands."

Heather clicked a remote and the monitor went dark. Despite whatever authority she and Sturgis had at Q2, they were both just Yao's lackeys.

Sturgis stepped in front of the desk. "Each of you will continue the work you've started at home. We'll provide accommodations and rations. The menu may not be gourmet, but I promise that you will not go hungry. Your ankle bracelets will keep you from leaving the compound, but as long as you comply with instructions and attempt nothing foolish, the three of you may work together in the lab and socialize around mealtimes."

"And if we don't… comply?" I asked.

Sturgis sighed loudly. "If any of you attempt to leave, resist direction, or try to communicate with the outside in any way,

I assure you that things will become significantly more unpleasant for you."

He walked to the door and nodded to Heather. "Dr. Avanair will now outline the next steps of your assignments."

"I don't know who you all think you are," I shouted with rage, "but you can't do this!"

Heather was silent for a moment and then sat in a chair directly across from me. "I can understand that you're upset, Bryce. That you all are. But I urge you to consider your situation. Try to remember that you're still contributing to an amazing discovery that will change the world for generations to come."

"I hope they're paying you a fortune," muttered Rachel.

Heather bit her lip, but she didn't answer. She just walked to the front of the room and pulled three laptops from a drawer. "We should get started. I had your machines brought here to the lab, so you can continue where we left off. Being together physically will actually make it easier to coordinate your individual coding sequences. The strands are coming together. Soon we'll move to the main lab with Mr. Fitz to complete the initiative."

CHAPTER TWENTY-SEVEN_

That's how it was for a while. Three weeks, I think, but it could have been more. The days all ran together. Each was the same—wake, shower and dress, eat, then work in the lab for hours. They allowed us thirty minutes up on the roof after each meal, a welcome chance to see the sky and breathe fresh air. But there was nowhere to go. The roof was five stories up. We might as well have been on the platform of the water tower, just without the view of Milton or the promise of returning home.

I thought about making a run for it each time we'd leave the computer lab, but I knew I'd never make it. The mountain was no place to be without food or supplies, and the ankle tracker would bring them swooping down on me in minutes. The only glimmer of hope was that I found a way to continue hiding bits of code. They didn't seem to be able to trace my secret drop file. At this point, I could only hope that when they went to run the machine, it would stall their cooling systems and prevent the quantum accelerators from functioning.

Rachel and I had made a practice of walking loops around the outer edge of the roof. It felt like doing laps in gym class. But Charlie never joined us. He usually sat on a bench staring blankly into the forest. He did his work in the lab, but the rest of the time he was only a shell of his former, jovial self. His will was broken.

"I heard Avanair speaking with Fitz," said Rachel, one clear day after lunch. "It's getting very close."

I nodded as we passed Charlie's bench and started another lap. "Yeah. I think they're about to bring us down to the main lab to bring the final strands together."

"And then what? Where does that leave us?"

"They'll need to test it," I answered. "See if it really crosses into the virtual world." It seemed crazy to even say it aloud, but at this point, I knew that was their plan.

"Could it really work?" asked Rachel. "It seems so theoretical when I'm coding. It's hard to believe they can actually connect into *Final Kingdom.* No one's ever done anything close to that before."

I nodded. "It could. I guess it's like sending a man to the moon. Or another world."

Rachel let out a long breath. "The virtual world."

OUR WORKSTATIONS WERE SPREAD across the same long table, separated enough to be comfortable, but close enough to see what the others were doing. Heather watched us from behind her own monitor, sitting at the front of the room like a proctor during the SATs. I didn't think she was a programmer like us, but she seemed to project-manage each of the assignments before passing them on to Fitz's other teams to implement.

She'd announced that we'd be moving to the main lab the next morning. She didn't say why, but a sense of urgency and excitement had been building for days—the bridge was nearly finished.

I pictured working in the larger lab. Fitz was a fat slob, but he held power over Sturgis and Heather. Eden was his brain-child, and despite everyone's clear disgust for his slovenly style, they all treated him with respect. The few times I'd interacted with him since being held prisoner, I'd noticed the gleam in his eye when he spoke of the work. He may not have had the same motivation as Yao, but he possessed a similar lust for power.

I was lost in thought about Fitz and the Eden project when it happened. A shock, like a pulse of electricity, shot through my keyboard. It was a sharp pinch, like a bee sting, and my hands jerked back from the keys. I coughed and tried to stay inconspicuous. Heather glanced up at me briefly but then continued her work. I looked down the row, but Rachel and Charlie seemed lost in their regular flow.

I turned back to my laptop. What could have zapped me? The machine plugged into a standard electrical outlet. A power surge would have affected the others along the same circuit, and neither of them had reacted to anything. I scrolled back up my most recent code string to see if the surge had affected anything. All seemed in order—until the strangest thing happened.

The lines on my screen seemed to twist and turn. Almost as if the LCD screen had rippled, which was impossible. I bounced my eyes to the front of the room to ensure Heather was occupied and then leaned closer. A message flashed.

Keep working. Don't look up.

Who is this? I typed back. It could be a trap laid by Yao, Sturgis, or maybe even Heather from the front of the room. They could be baiting me, trying to see what I might reveal.

I glanced again at Charlie and Rachel, but they seemed oblivious.

It's Tyler, a new message flashed.

I caught my breath. *What are you doing? They're going to detect you,* I typed.

No, they won't. We found a safe way to cut into your system, but we have to be quick. Listen carefully. We know they have taken you. Are you safe?

I considered the many ways to answer that question, but in the strictest, most immediate sense of the word, I was.

Yes, I replied.

Who else is with you?

Rachel and Charlie.

What is the status of Eden?

It's nearly ready. Only a few more days.

You have to stop them.

A bead of sweat dripped off my forehead. How could Tyler be sending me these messages? And if it really was him, he was taking a big chance that no one else could see my computer screen. I expected Heather or someone else inside the building to storm over and haul me away at any moment.

I don't know how to send more code, I replied.

No time for that. We need you to sabotage the project.

Sabotage? What did he expect me to do, set off a bomb in the building? This was madness.

Heather scooted her chair back from the table and my body froze.

I have to keep working, I typed.

Even if they couldn't see his communications, if I didn't keep advancing in the programming sequence, they would surely notice that. We had to wrap this up.

Pay attention. I'm going to send a virus. Download it to a portable memory drive. Get to the central lab mainframe and upload the virus into the Eden Machine. It's the only way to stop them.

I stared at the screen. I didn't have a portable drive, and even if I did, how was I supposed to get it to the mainframe without anyone noticing?

Bryce, can you do that?

I don't know. Let me think. I don't have a portable drive.

Find one. Do you have your laptop at night?

Yes.

Good. Log on tonight at midnight. I'll send you the virus then.

I'll try.

Be careful, Bryce. There's not much time.

The screen rippled once more, then went back to normal. I blinked, wondering if I'd just imagined it all. Rachel must have noticed that I'd stopped typing.

"What's wrong?" she whispered.

I shook my head. "I'll tell you later."

I tried to concentrate on my code, but my mind was spinning a hundred miles an hour. Would a virus really be able to stop Eden?

CHAPTER TWENTY-EIGHT_

I pulled Rachel aside on the roof after lunch and explained the messages from Tyler.

"What?" she exclaimed. "How is that possible?"

I put my finger to my lips. "I don't know, but it happened, and now we have to do something. I think Fitz's computer connects directly to the Eden mainframe. We might get near it when we move to the main lab."

"Where are you going to get a virus? Tyler can't send it to you in a FedEx envelope." Rachel glanced up at the overcast sky. "Is he going to drop it to you here on the roof from a drone?"

I laughed nervously but shook my head. "He wants me to download it onto a portable drive tonight."

"Like a memory stick?"

"Yeah, I think so. But there's one problem."

"There's a lot more than one, but what?"

"I don't have a memory stick."

"I know where you can get one." Charlie's voice surprised us. I hadn't noticed him walk up behind us.

I eyed him curiously. He hadn't been himself, and I didn't know what to expect from him. "Get one what?"

"A memory stick. Isn't that what you said you needed?"

"Charlie," Rachel said slowly, "this has to be kept secret. You can't say anything."

For one of the first times since they captured us, Charlie grinned like he had when we'd first met during orientation. "I got it. Cool your jets."

Maybe he'd finally gotten over the shock of what had happened. Maybe Eden's nearing completion was waking him up. Or maybe it was hope—the possibility, even if just a sliver, that we might stop the madness spinning all around us—that we could be part of a solution, not just unwilling accomplices to something terrible.

"You have a memory stick?" I asked.

"No," Charlie replied, "but I saw one in the drawer of Avanair's desk in our lab."

"Doesn't she keep that locked?" asked Rachel.

"Only when she's not there."

I sighed. "But she's always there, Charlie."

"That's why we need a diversion."

"Like what?" asked Rachel.

He grinned again. "Leave that to me. Just be ready to jump up and swipe the stick when it happens. It's in her top right drawer, but you'll only have a moment to grab it."

I thought about the plan. If Charlie could get Heather out of the room for even a few seconds, I might be able to get to the drawer and take the memory stick, if it even existed.

Rachel seemed to work the timeline through in her mind. "If you get the stick this afternoon, you can download the virus tonight, and then we can take it to the mainframe tomorrow."

There were a lot of "ifs" to the plan, but we were out of options. There was no "Plan B."

Charlie never said what his diversion would be, just that we'd know it when it took place. So I tried to be alert and ready while I programmed, but when it finally happened, it caught me by surprise.

Thud.

Charlie's head snapped down on the table, smack on top of his keyboard. Blood spurted in all directions.

"Oh my god, Charlie!" Rachel exclaimed, jumping from her chair.

"What's going on?" Heather moved swiftly to our table.

"Ah… my nose," Charlie moaned, pulling his shirt up from his waist to absorb some of the blood. Purposeful or not, it looked like he'd truly broken his nose.

"I think he fell asleep and banged his head on the table," cried Rachel.

Heather didn't seem to know what to do first. "Well, stand up, *Chaalee*!" she yelled. She looked faint as she ushered him toward the door. Charlie moaned loudly, but amidst the confusion, he turned and stared at me through his hands as if to say *what are you waiting for?*

The chaotic scene had even distracted me, but I quickly jumped to attention and calculated the best path to the desk as Heather ushered Charlie out the doorway and called for support. I raced to the front of the room, yanking at the top right drawer.

It was locked.

Panic filled my brain. Heather was still in the hall, but she could return any second. Charlie was carrying on like someone had speared him through the heart. I searched the desk frantically, my eyes finally landing on a small, bronze key attached to Heather's access card. I prayed it was the correct one as I grabbed it and pushed it into the keyhole. The lock turned, and I slid the drawer open. Sitting on top of another laptop were two slim memory sticks. I grabbed one, slipping it into my pocket, then quickly re-locked the drawer and placed the key and access card back where they had been on the desk.

I reached my workstation just as Heather reentered the room. Blood was splattered across her arms and blouse. It was disgusting, but I almost smiled. She looked like she was about to combust.

"Stand up, both of you!" she hissed. "You're to wait back in your rooms while I get—while we clean up this mess."

Rachel and I just gawked at her, standing at the front of the room like an extra from a slasher film.

"Don't just stand there. Move it!" she cried.

We picked up our laptops and sped out of the room. A sly smile slipped briefly across Rachel's lips. I felt it too. For the first time in what seemed like forever, our glimmer of hope was growing.

I DIDN'T DARE FALL ASLEEP. NOT that I could have if I'd tried. I watched the shadows from the moonlight drift across the ceiling of my room. Just before midnight, I slid from the bed, discreetly grabbing the laptop as I walked to the bathroom. It seemed appropriate to be hiding in the bathroom to connect with Tyler, since that was the place I'd first heard his name.

I prayed that Charlie had been correct about the bathroom being free from cameras all those weeks ago. I didn't know if Q2 would monitor unusual late-night activity on my laptop, but I had no choice. If Tyler's first message had broken through their firewall undetected, surely he could do it again. I realized too that this could be the best time to share the passcode for my hidden sequences. I'd put the passcode on Maggie's pendant for insurance against everyone, but now I had to trust Tyler. Everything was banking on it.

As the clock turned to midnight, another ripple shot across the laptop screen. I lifted my hands from the keys to avoid a shock.

A message appeared. *Ready?*

Yes.

Save this file directly to the portable drive. Remember, you must upload the virus directly into the Eden mainframe.

Got it. Wait, I need to tell you something.

But he didn't reply to the last part of my message. All he wrote back was: *Good luck, Bryce.*

A link appeared for a file transfer. There was no further window to chat with Tyler, so I plugged the memory stick into the same side port I'd used for the mirroring device back in my bedroom, then clicked *Accept*. It took just two minutes for the files to load. Communication with Tyler seemed to be gone, so I ejected the stick and closed the computer, flushing the toilet to conceal my reason for going in the bathroom. I tiptoed back to the bed, slipping my computer back onto the table and hiding the stick under the mattress.

I tried to sleep, but it was impossible. There was too much

in my brain. I kept picturing how I could enter the lab and access Fitz's machine without being seen. It was a crazy plan, but one that had to work.

CHAPTER TWENTY-NINE_

At breakfast, Rachel caught my eye to see if everything had gone according to plan overnight. I nodded, trying not to self-consciously touch the thin drive in my pocket. If anyone searched me, I'd be finished. We hadn't seen Charlie after his nose incident, but he eventually arrived in the breakfast room, wearing a splint and several strips of white tape across his face.

"Oh, Charlie," said Rachel. His left eye was black and blue. He looked like he'd just been mugged or had been on the wrong side of a street fight.

"Don't worry. It feels worse than it looks." He laughed but then winced in pain.

"I've got to hand it you," I said. "When you create a diversion, you go all out." I patted him on the back gently. "Thanks."

"Did you get it?" Charlie whispered.

I nodded just as Heather came into the room. She spotted Charlie and shot him a death glare. He'd never been on her good side, and I doubted she'd ever forgive him for covering her in blood.

"Let's finish up, people," Heather ordered. "We're moving to the central lab this morning. Despite his many vices, Mr. Fitz isn't one to tolerate lateness."

We carried our laptops and took the elevator to the bottom floor. I'd only been to the main lab once, during orientation, and the scope of the project again amazed me. We were far from the only team working to bring Eden to life.

Fitz assigned us to a table several rows from his desk. It was too far from the mainframe. Fitz was always at his desk, and people were buzzing throughout the room. It would be impossible to get to the access panel unnoticed.

"As you know, we've had teams of programmers working on this project for months," Fitz proclaimed. "But your particular team was handling a very pesky problem."

"A missing person's report?" I said caustically.

Fitz frowned but ignored me. "In order to bridge the digital frontier, to cross into the virtual world, we must alter an object's molecular structure. We accomplish this feat by accelerating quantum mass to what amounts to nearly twice the speed of light, more than 500,000 miles per second.

"Eden successfully reached that incredible velocity some time ago; however, we've struggled to counterbalance the abundance of generated heat energy. Thanks to your work, our coolant program now properly absorbs the heat and redistributes it back into the power generators. As a result, the quantum accelerators can operate with no danger of combusting."

He grinned at us proudly, his ugly teeth on wide display.

"It stymied us for quite some time, I'm willing to admit, but thanks to your hard work, we have a solution."

"You're not welcome," I muttered, feeling more defeated than ever.

"Ingrates," Fitz grunted. "No wonder you got yourselves locked up. You wouldn't recognize a world-changing idea if it hit you in the face." He glanced at Charlie's bandaged nose and chuckled. His stomach growled loudly. "Changing the world makes me hungry. I'll be right back. I've listed your final coding sequences on your screens." He walked past us to the door before turning. "So get to work!"

I froze, glancing back and forth with my eyes. Could it be that easy? There were dozens of other nameless programmers in the back of the room, but they didn't seem to be paying any attention. This might be my only chance.

I nodded to Rachel and Charlie as I slipped from my chair. I slowly stepped up the aisle toward the mainframe. I pulled the drive from my pocket and knelt down, searching for the access panel to the Eden's inner core. A clear plastic guard fit over a series of access ports with colored lights. That was it.

I shifted the data stick into my other hand, reached down, and raised the plastic cover, spinning the drive stick in my fingers so the ports matched up. I almost had it.

The drive was only inches from the port when a siren sounded. An alarm screeched across the room. I jerked my hand back as a thin, metal cover automatically slid across the access panel, blocking the ports to the mainframe.

I turned around. Charlie was at Fitz's desk, his hand hovering next to a wide switch. He'd flipped an emergency fail-safe. That's what had set off the alarm and closed the access panel. What was happening?

I stared up at him in shock. "Why?" was all I could utter.

"Charlie, what are you doing?" Rachel called, racing over to us.

The main doors to the lab swung open as Fitz, Sturgis, and Heather stormed into the room. They marched over to us.

"Turns out I wasn't that hungry after all," said Fitz. He laughed obnoxiously. "First time ever." He snatched the memory stick from my hand. "You didn't think I was that naive, did you, kid? Besides, whatever you had on that drive wouldn't work on my machine, anyway. Probably from Hendrickson, right? Eden is far too sophisticated for that Boy Scout's simple-minded traps."

Charlie stepped next to Sturgis and Heather as we watched in disbelief.

"You traitor!" Rachel cried, looking like she was about to explode.

Charlie finally met my gaze. "Don't look at me like that, Bryce."

"Why did you do it?" I said meekly, feeling more defeated than angry.

He shook his head. "They interrogated me at the nurse's clinic. They forced me to talk. But it doesn't matter, guys, I swear to you. They already knew everything. It was only a matter of time. And besides, it's too late. Eden is done." He stared at his shoes, but when he looked back at me, his voice cracked, and I thought I saw a tear in his eye. "They said they would kill my little cousins. What was I supposed to do?"

I closed my eyes. A wave of resignation swept through my body. That drive was our last hope. It was over.

"It was a smart decision, Mr. Kilroy," said Sturgis. "It's nice to see at least one of you making a sound judgment. I expected so much more from this group, but you never can tell who will crack under the pressure or fail to see the big picture."

"You're sick," Rachel hissed.

"Think what you want," Sturgis replied. "Mr. Yao will arrive shortly. Tonight, Eden will be operational."

They took Rachel and me to our rooms. I don't know what happened to Charlie. Maybe he was one of them now. Did they turn him after he broke his nose, or before? After everything we'd been through, what had been real and what was just an act? The blood had been real, but maybe he just couldn't take it anymore. Sturgis said Rachel and I had cracked, but we were the only ones in this place who had held strong.

Our doors didn't open for dinner, but around eight, Heather appeared with the beefy man who'd grabbed me in my driveway.

"Secure his wrists," she ordered.

"Where are we going?" I asked, as the goon zip-tied my hands together.

"There's something we want you to see," said Heather.

I stumbled against the wall when fat-hands pushed me toward the hallway. "I've seen all I need to see."

Heather turned to me as the elevator sank to the ground floor. "Despite what you may think, Bryce, I am not a monster. If you'd only been open to seeing the bigger picture, you could have been a part of so much… more." She placed her hand on my cheek, but I turned away, refusing to match her stare.

"Foolish to the end," Heather muttered coldly as the doors slid open.

A crowd was already gathered in the lab around the Eden mainframe. Rachel was there, her hands bound like mine. Charlie stood with Sturgis and Fitz, both looking like they were waiting for something. Or someone. Finally, Sturgis nodded toward the skybox in the back of the room. Moments later, Yao entered, his assistant trailing several steps behind.

"Everything is ready, Mr. Yao," Fitz declared, his voice loud in giddy anticipation.

Yao walked between our two groups, tapping his cane on the floor as he paused in front of Rachel and me. He clucked his tongue while shaking his head, then continued to the machine.

"Excellent work, Mr. Fitz."

"You won't get away with this," Rachel cried. She tried to move forward, but the beefy man held her back.

"Oh, but I already have, Miss Kelly. Eden is fully functional. There is no turning back, despite your feeble attempts at sabotage. While I admire your passion, it's foolishly misplaced. You will learn the hard way, as so many others have over the centuries—there is no standing in the way of the Red Dragon. Despite your disloyalty, I thought it only fitting that you both see our creation put to the test."

His assistant pulled out a chair, and Yao sat facing the machine. He waved his hand through the air, like a conductor to an orchestra. "Whenever you're ready, Mr. Fitz."

Fitz rubbed his thick palms together as he moved to his workstation. "Mr. Kilroy, would you please assist me since the rest of your team seems to be indisposed?"

Charlie moved to the workstation next to Fitz's desk and followed a series of instructions. The giant wall monitor flashed on, displaying a wide desert plateau that I immediately recognized as a level in *Kingdom.* It was flat, with only a single thick rock formation towering into the sky like a giant sculpture in the shape of a capital letter T.

With Fitz and Charlie at the controls, the silver Eden Machine sprang to life, bathing the room in a green glow and starting a gentle, rhythmic humming sound. A panel rose like the door of an exotic sports car, revealing a small chamber the size of a shower stall.

At Fitz's signal, four strong men stepped forward carrying a square electronic device. It looked like a portable generator, the kind I'd seen Mr. Janakowski from down the street use after a storm had knocked out power to the neighborhood. They placed it in the empty chamber and moved quickly away. Was it some kind of communications device?

As the chamber door lowered, Fitz motioned to Heather. She handed dark goggles to each person in the room. I thought she might skip us, but she strapped them over Rachel's head and then mine. She looked into my eyes, her face darkened by the lenses. "I want you to appreciate what you're missing out on."

"Ready when you are, Mr. Yao," called Fitz.

Yao leaned forward in his chair, resting his chin on his cane. His narrow face looked like a wrinkled bug thanks to the oversized dark goggles. "Proceed."

Fitz nodded, and lights began flashing around the room. A countdown message appeared in the center of the screen on the wall.

Initiation commencing in ten seconds, it read.

I felt my breath tighten. I hoped the code gaps I'd inserted into Eden's cooling sequences should be enough to bring the machine to a crashing halt, but it was just a theory. I'd never accessed the full schematic. Another system could override my gap and continue the operation, or they may have found my omission and corrected it.

The lights turned brighter, and a dark green smoke curled inside the chamber. The Eden Machine's smooth central cylinder lifted from the floor on sturdy supports at both ends. Like a high-tech cement mixer, the silver construct began to turn, over and over, but then, incredibly, also side to side, as if defying the laws of physics. It spun like one of the wild rides at the county fair that I'd never had the nerve to try.

But then, just as the machine began to accelerate, a red light flashed across the giant wall screen. The movement rapidly ground to a halt.

Warning! Cooling systems inoperable. Quantum accelerators may overheat. Password required.

Fitz cursed and slammed his palm against his desk.

My stomach turned upside down. It had worked, but now I wondered about the consequence for what I'd done.

Fitz yanked off his goggles, his face ablaze. He turned toward me, lips curled back like a savage beast. "What did you do?" he growled.

I clenched my teeth, resolved not to speak. They couldn't kill me if they wanted the passcode. It was my insurance.

Yao raised his hand at Fitz, like he was calling off a rabid dog. He calmly removed his goggles and stepped forward, his cane squeaking against the floor. He lifted my goggles onto my forehead, and then stared into my eyes.

"Your tenacity continues to impress, Bryce. It's a quality

that drew us to you from the beginning. But now the jig is up, you might say. Give me the passcode."

I stared past him, motionless. I didn't care what they did to me. I wasn't giving it to them.

Yao's expression hardened. "Very well then." He nodded at the man holding Rachel. He shoved her forward. Heather Avanair pulled out a gun and pushed it against Rachel's temple.

I suddenly realized my error. They didn't have to touch me. As long as they had people I cared about, I was their pawn.

"Don't do it, Bryce," Rachel pleaded. "It's not worth it."

Yao clucked his tongue. "Consider your next move carefully, Bryce. For even if Rachel is willing to sacrifice herself, your loved ones back in Milton might prove an even greater motivation. Either way, you will give me what I want."

I closed my eyes as they welled up with tears. They had me cornered.

"The passcode," Yao repeated. "Now."

My body felt numb. I nodded faintly and walked to Fitz's console. I entered the password. The warning lights were replaced with a new message on the screen.

Activation commencing in 10 seconds.

"Thank you," Yao said calmly. He repositioned his goggles. "Proceed, Mr. Fitz."

Heather lowered the gun, and Rachel and I were moved back with the others. Everyone reattached their goggles.

The Eden Machine again rose from its supports, green lights blurring as it moved faster and faster. I pictured it spinning out of control and flying across the room like a wounded fighter jet, but it held its position. Just when it seemed like it couldn't spin any faster, an enormous burst of light shot from its center. A wave of energy pulsed across the room, knocking me backward. Even with the dark goggles, I blinked in the brightness. Splotches of green filled my vision as my eyes readjusted.

When I regained focus, I saw Fitz and the others removing their goggles. The machine gradually slowed, reducing its spin until it rested back on its supports. When it stopped, the crowd was silent. Fitz punched at the controls, and the door slowly rose. The chamber was empty.

Where was the communicator device? Had it disintegrated? My mind raced through the possibilities as everyone's attention turned to the wall. Fitz toggled the giant monitor's view across the orange desert landscape, zooming in closer toward the T-shaped boulder.

Just past the base of the boulder, sitting on the sandy desert floor, was the generator-shaped communications machine. It was inside *Kingdom*. They had done it.

A slow, steady clap was the first sound. Yao rose from his seat as the room erupted into celebration.

"Congratulations, everyone," Yao cried. "We have achieved a first for humankind. We have bridged the digital frontier. Together we have crossed into a new dimension and taken the first step in a new phase of human existence."

Rachel and I stood motionless amidst the celebrations. We had failed. There was truly no stopping them now. Charlie, too, stood silently, his eyes transfixed on the desert scene on the monitor.

Yao turned back to the machine, his face suddenly serious. "How long until we can make a second transmission, Mr. Fitz?"

Fitz pulled up a new screen on the mainframe. "The generators need at least five hours to recharge. We should be ready at full strength first thing in the morning."

Yao nodded and turned toward us. I expected another self-righteous speech about honor and the coming dominance of the East, but he just nodded to the man behind me.

"Take them away," he ordered.

CHAPTER THIRTY_

Nights used to be for sleeping. That was before I sold my soul to Q2 and the cursed Eden Machine. Now, even without a late-night assignment, I lay awake, staring at the ceiling and thinking of home. What were Mom, Dad, Zach, and Maggie doing? What did they think had happened to me? Did they hate me? Had they already moved on? Were they searching for me? There was no way to know.

That night was worse than most. Yao's Eden Machine had bridged the real and virtual worlds. Charlie had betrayed us. Tyler had said JOSHUA was being developed in cooperation with the government. Maybe they would send a Special Forces unit for a late-night rescue like in the movies. But they couldn't know that we'd been discovered or that I had failed in my attempt to feed the virus into the mainframe. Now, without my laptop, we had no way to contact each other. I was literally at the end of the road. That little glimmer of hope that we'd clung to was now completely extinguished.

As I lay there pondering how they might kill me, my room's security lock beeped. The latch slowly turned. A figure slid silently through the doorway and then into the bathroom. Was I dreaming? Were they coming to haul me away in the cover of night, just like the other poor soul who'd once called to me through the vent in desperation?

I lay motionless, searching the room with my eyes for a weapon to defend myself. I would go down fighting. What did I have to lose?

"Bryce," a faint whisper called from the bathroom.

That seemed like a confusing tactic for a midnight assassin. I sat up and squinted into the darkness. "Who's there?"

"It's me," the voice whispered back.

"Charlie?" What was he doing in my room? How had he gotten out of his? And why was he hiding in the bathroom?

"Get dressed." His voice was barely audible from across the room. "I'm getting you out of here."

I hesitated, but then I pulled on my clothes. My blood began to boil. He was a turncoat and a coward. I considered punching him in the face when I rounded the corner. Most likely he was leading me out to a late-night firing squad in the woods.

I crept to the bathroom door. "What are you doing here?"

"I told you. I'm breaking you out." He held up a keycard. "I swiped it off Fitz's desk after the Eden test. Everyone was too excited to notice." He slid along the wall and opened the hallway door. "I'll explain later, but we have to get Rachel. Follow me. And be silent."

I still hesitated, but he placed a gentle hand on my shoulder. "I know you have no reason to, but you have to trust me, Bryce." His face was only inches from mine, close enough to see his eyes in the darkness. They looked sincere. "Please. Let me help you."

I knew that I could either follow Charlie into the dark hallway or wait for them to haul me from my bed. It was really no choice at all. I nodded and stepped forward.

We slipped through the hallway to Rachel's door. Charlie waved the keycard over the lock pad. The electronic beep echoed down the hallway like we'd dropped a glass jar. We froze, waiting for any repercussions, but it stayed quiet. Charlie turned the handle and slipped into her bathroom the same way he had mine.

"Rachel," I whispered from the doorway. I didn't get an answer. I didn't want to risk being seen on camera, but I had no choice. I moved silently toward her outline under the covers and then shook her shoulder gently.

Her eyes bulged open wide in surprise, but I pressed my hand against her mouth to stifle her scream. I held a finger to my lips, then slowly pulled my palm from her mouth once she seemed to register that it was me.

"How did you get in here?" she whispered.

"I'll explain, but right now you have to get dressed. Quickly."

She rubbed her eyes, but then nodded and slid out of bed. I turned and tried not to look as she pulled on her clothes. When she tapped my shoulder to say that she was ready, we crept toward the door.

She froze when Charlie's shadow emerged from the bathroom. "What the hell?"

"Just come on," I urged, taking her hand as Charlie pulled the door open. "Trust me."

Charlie seemed to know where he was going, but he paused at the elevator bank. "Too risky." He pointed to the stairwell, and we descended to the lower level. The creak of the stairwell's heavy fire door at the basement level made more noise than we wanted, but still no one seemed to hear.

Rachel pulled back when we reached the entrance to the main computer lab. "Okay, stop. What are we doing here?" She pointed at Charlie. "What is *he* doing here?"

Charlie swiped the card across the access panel and opened the door. "Not out here. Inside. I'll explain. I promise." He pushed the door open, and we both begrudgingly followed him inside.

The large room was strangely quiet in the middle of the night. I'd never seen it without workers, and the rows of empty workstations and equipment cast an eerie glow.

"All right," I said, crossing my arms. "We've followed you down here. Now start talking."

"We have to get out of here," Charlie answered. "It's only a matter of time until they take us out. We have to hide."

I lowered my eyebrows. "Sure, but where? We'll never get out of here." I pointed to the tracking bracelet around my ankle. "They'll be on us in no time. We've been over this."

"Why did you bring us down here to the lab?" asked Rachel, eyeing the quiet room suspiciously. "I thought you were on *their* side now."

"Don't you see?" Charlie answered. "This is the only place where we *can* escape."

Rachel shook her head. "I think he's lost his mind."

"No, I haven't. Think about it. We all know *Kingdom* inside and out. There must be thousands of places inside all the levels to hide. Millions, maybe." Charlie pointed at the Eden Machine. "And now we have a way to get there."

I rubbed my face, trying to clear my brain. "And then

what? We're supposed to live inside a video game for the rest of our lives? What kind of existence is that?"

Charlie shook his head. "Not forever. Just until the competition gets their bridge up and running."

Rachel and I exchanged uneasy looks. We'd never talked to him about JOSHUA.

"I'm not blind," Charlie added. "I've seen you guys scheming. You're feeding code to the other side, aren't you? They must be close behind. They can beam us back home with their machine. We can contact them through the communicator."

"What communicator?" asked Rachel.

"The device they sent across in the test. It was a console for direct contact between the two worlds and a way to control the coordinates for return trips. We'll use it to get back once their bridge is online."

"And if that takes a while?" I asked. "What then?"

"In the meantime, we lie low. We wait."

"What if they come after us?" asked Rachel. "I mean, *if* we make it across. What keeps them from just following us?"

"Didn't you hear Fitz after the test?" Charlie replied. "He said the quantum generators need at least five hours to recharge between transmissions."

"Has it been five hours?" I asked.

Charlie glanced at a clock on the desk and shrugged. "Pretty much."

"Pretty much?" said Rachel. "What if it doesn't work?"

"It'll work, Rachel," said Charlie.

"But can't they just wait five hours and come after us?" I asked, trying to think through the details.

Charlie grinned. "The keycard wasn't the only thing I swiped off Fitz's desk." He handed me the memory stick.

"Once we get across, we feed the virus into the system from the other side. If it's everything Tyler told you it is, it should knock Eden's bridge out of commission, at least for a little while."

He was quiet for a few moments, letting us process his plan.

Rachel spoke first. "You know, it might be just crazy enough to work."

I looked at her in surprise. "What?"

She nodded. "What are our other choices? Charlie's right, they're never going to let us out of here. They don't need our programming skills any longer now that Eden is functional. We were always just a means to an end for Yao and the rest of them. They probably planned to dispose of us all along, even if we had cooperated."

I'd never thought of that.

"Bryce." Charlie stared at me, his face serious. "I get that you don't trust me. Hell, if I were you I wouldn't either. I'm sorry. I can't change what I did. I swear, on the lives of my little cousins—I'll make it up to you. But if we don't do this, we're as good as dead in the morning anyhow."

"You mean *we're* dead," I said, gesturing at me and Rachel.

Charlie waved his hand. "Me too, probably. What do they need me for? Another body won't make a difference to them. It's easier if they start with a clean slate. But we don't have time to sit here and argue. Follow me or don't, but I'm doing this."

He walked up the aisle to the Eden Machine followed by Rachel.

I knew he was right. We had no choice. "Do you even know how to run this?" I asked, coming up behind them. The operation console was dark, but Eden's green lights still glowed ominously.

Charlie nodded. "I was watching Fitz. The final coding for the quantum accelerators was the only thing holding them up. Activation is a fairly simple execute function. We don't need to touch the coordinates. They're still set on the desert inside *Kingdom* where they sent the communicator."

Rachel looked up at the screen. "So we have to live in the desert?"

Charlie shook his head. "We can go anywhere we want to once we're inside."

I thought about the hours I'd spent playing *Kingdom* back home with Zach. Another worry flashed in my mind. "What about everything else inside *Kingdom*?"

"Everything else?" Charlie asked, sitting in Fitz's chair. He typed quickly into the mainframe. "You mean the other players? I'm not sure how that will work, but I assume we'd be able to interact with them."

"No," I said. "I mean things native to the game."

"Oh my god, you're right," said Rachel. "I didn't even think about that. The Rangers, night cats, sentinels, and everything else they designed to hunt down game players. That was fun when it was just virtual, but I don't actually want to meet any of them."

"I don't know, but at least there we have a chance at survival. We still have no other choice." Charlie stared up at us. "Are you with me?"

I took a deep breath and looked at Rachel. "I am if you are."

"Let's do it."

I nodded to Charlie. "Ready."

"Awesome." He pushed two more buttons, and the chamber door rose upward.

Rachel peered into the chamber. "Is there room for all three of us?"

"How are you going to operate it and get in at the same time?" I asked.

Charlie pointed at the control panel. "There's a timed release for the countdown once the coordinates are set. I can start it before the doors shut. I think I'll have time. But we have to hurry. They might monitor these systems. They could be here any minute."

I took Rachel's hand, and we stepped into the chamber while Charlie finished at the controls. The lights pulsed like we had stepped inside a living organism. An image of the desert plateau and some numbered coordinates were on a square-shaped monitor near our waists. It looked like the same location where they'd sent the communicator in the test.

As the motor warmed, a steady revving sound filled the room. Inside the chamber it sounded like a jet engine coming to life. A green mist crept up from the floor. If they hadn't known we were here before, they'd definitely know now. It wouldn't be long till someone came. Rachel held my arm tightly as we looked out into the lab. We had to hurry.

Charlie was still at Fitz's workstation, typing madly at the keyboard. "What are you waiting for?" I yelled over the roar.

Charlie held up a finger, standing at the keyboard, glancing back and forth at the screen. The green fog spilled out from the open doorway and into the lab like a primordial soup at the dawn of creation. Maybe that was why Yao had named it Eden. As if God was just an overzealous programmer, a mad scientist whose technology had birthed a new world.

Lights flashed across the lab, and I could barely hear a countdown sequence over the speakers. The wall screen counted backwards from sixty seconds. Had the quantum generators had enough time to recharge, or was it too soon?

"I got it!" Charlie leapt from the workstation and stepped toward us. Rachel and I pushed toward the back of the chamber to make as much room as possible. We were really doing this.

I waved him ahead. "Come on!"

But just then the doors flew open in the back of the room. Fitz appeared and ran up the aisle between the rows of work-stations. His eyes were wild, like a madman, and his giant arms flailed as he moved toward us. Sturgis and Heather were right behind him, followed by Yao, who stepped through the doorway much more slowly with his cane.

Charlie looked over his shoulder. He saw them coming, but they were still far away. He glanced up at the screen. Only seconds remained on the countdown.

He turned back to us as he broke into a run toward the chamber. They were too late. He was going to make it. We all were. To what end, there was no telling, but we'd be together and away from this place. Come what may, we would figure it out.

We made eye contact, a grin spreading across Charlie's face as he looked at me.

But suddenly his expression changed. His body tumbled forward.

Behind him, Heather lowered a gun. Yao's lips formed a thin smile.

"Charlie!" screamed Rachel. She lunged forward to go to him, but I held her back. In the struggle, we crashed against the monitor on the wall. Out of the corner of my eye, I saw a cascade of images like numbers on a spinning roulette wheel. I looked back into the lab.

The timer was gone.

It was too late.

The chamber door began to automatically lower.

Charlie raised his head weakly. He nodded at us, as if to confirm that he'd made amends for his betrayal, just as he'd promised. Then he sank down against the floor as the chamber door closed, sealing us in.

CHAPTER THIRTY-ONE_

We pressed our hands against the clear inner panel of the Eden Machine. We strained to see the lab, but the green mist from the chamber floor had now thickened into a fog. I could barely make out the image that had settled on the destination monitor near my waist—a farm, fields, barns—what was that?

It grew harder and harder to breathe. Rachel began to cough, and I could feel the gas seeping into my lungs. I couldn't see Sturgis, Fitz, Heather, Yao… or Charlie. What were they thinking? That they'd won? Maybe they had.

I remembered during the test how the machine had spun faster and faster, up and over, side to side. But inside, despite the brightness and rising heat, the chamber felt completely still. Rachel pressed against me. We held each other tightly, as if the harder we squeezed, the more of a chance we had to make it—flying to the edge of the world and beyond.

The mechanics of what was happening flashed through my brain. Fitz had said the Eden Machine spun at an incredible rate to accelerate quantum particles above light speed—up to 500,000 miles per second. That was enough to bridge dimensions and send us crashing into the virtual world like a baseball shattering a pane of glass.

Sweat poured off my body as the temperatures rose. The communicator could likely withstand temperatures well above what a human being could. What if the heat was too extreme for a person? Would we burn up? Melt? Dissolve into nothingness?

I realized we weren't just holding each other anymore. The centrifugal force was pushing us closer, pressing against our very molecules. We couldn't move if we had wanted to. Then a burst of blinding green light filled the chamber, and the pressure instantly subsided. Now we were floating, separated and soaring through the air like birds. Rachel hovered next to me on a powerful surge of light.

And then we were sucked back in to the maelstrom, rushing through a tunnel of colors at an enormous speed, like on a waterslide. Pressure pushed in from all sides, crushing me, and I feared I would implode like a crumpled tin can. My molecules were redistributing. We might almost be there. I could sense it. It was working.

Then I was struggling for breath, desperate to pull air into my lungs. The communicator hadn't needed air, either. We were so close, yet it was suddenly hopeless. I stared ahead through the colorful tunnel. The doorway into the virtual world standing before me, waiting for me to enter, yet I could feel my consciousness drifting further and further away, like a body without gravity in outer space. I was suffocating, gasping for breath and yet unable to move.

But then everything stopped.

I plunged, headlong, into layers of hard but movable particles. I sunk deeper and deeper, the particles filling my lungs as I gasped for air. I opened my eyes, but my vision was clouded. I flailed my arms and the outside forces finally subsided. I was in something like quicksand. With every ounce of energy remaining in my body, I kicked my legs, desperately trying to pull myself in the direction I somehow knew was upward. But there was nothing to push against, and I made no progress.

Finally, my fingers grazed something metal. I heaved my other arm toward it, recognizing the familiar feel of a railing, like the ladder on the water tower. I pulled myself up, using the metal as a support, gradually moving higher. But my lungs were on fire. Whatever entrapped me had sucked out all the air, replacing it with a sandy dust that coated my lungs like poison. Yet I kept climbing, searching for a breath of air.

When I broke through the surface, my lungs sucked in the oxygen for what seemed like an eternity. I coughed, expelling dark chunks from my throat. My eyes opened, but particles floated through rays of light, still obscuring my vision. What was this place? What was I swimming in? Maybe this was the afterlife, or the in-between. Perhaps it was all just a ghastly dream.

I collapsed onto a platform at the top of the ladder. Gradually, my mind resuscitated and my vision cleared. I'd been swimming in an enormous bin of grain. A metal structure rose up around me, rounded but narrow, its walls made of gray and discolored sheet metal. It went high into the sky, to where light streamed in through a jagged opening in the roof. I was in a grain silo.

My memory raced back to the Eden chamber, to the

confusion as the door locked us in and the image of the farm on the screen. Somehow we'd changed coordinates. We hadn't landed on the desert plateau as planned. We were—

My eyes flashed to a movement in the grain below me. Something was there. A hand emerged, like a person sprouting from the ground. Rachel!

I leaped back into the grain, grasping the metal railing with one hand. I felt wildly through the sifting particles, following the fingers that had somehow reached the surface, down her wrist and arm, until I found her shoulder. I locked my hand under her arm and pulled with all my strength. Slowly she emerged through the sea of grain toward me and the surface. Her face appeared, but it was ghostly pale and covered in dust. She wasn't breathing. Was I too late?

I grasped her body at the waist, draped her over my shoulder, and climbed like a fireman up the ladder to the platform. I searched my memory for the CPR instruction I'd received in health class junior year and then reached into her mouth to pull away particles of grain that obstructed her airway. I began chest compressions, pausing every thirty times to push a long breath of air from my mouth toward her lungs. Over and over I pushed, harder and harder, against her chest.

As I began to fear she was gone, she lurched forward, coughing unnaturally, vomiting specks of blood and grain that had dangerously lined her windpipe. She turned and inhaled a long breath of air.

"Rachel, can you hear me?" I bent over her, brushing hair from her face.

Slowly she opened her eyes and recognized me. "Bryce? What happened? Where are we?"

I exhaled and leaned against the metal wall. "We did it," I answered.

Rachel coughed and pulled up on her elbows. "Are you sure?"

"Yes." I nodded. "It worked. We're inside *Kingdom*."

CHAPTER THIRTY-TWO_

We were glad to be alive, lying on that dirty wooden platform in the grain silo. Glad to have oxygen in our lungs and our molecules seemingly all back together in the right places. I pointed to a door several feet above us and we began to climb. I reached up and unlatched the handle of a three-foot square door in the silo. The handle turned, but nothing budged until I pulled myself higher and slammed my shoulder into the sheet metal like a linebacker. The metal gave way and flew outward on a hinge. Immediately, cool fresh air hit me in the face, and I paused to breathe the clean air into my dirty lungs.

Outside was a peaceful country setting, complete with a farmhouse, cow pasture, acres and acres of wheat, and a pond behind an old barn. A thin ladder ran down the outside of the silo, and I swung my legs through the opening before reaching back to grasp Rachel's hand and help her climb through. When we finally hit the ground, we both sank into the soft green grass and leaned against the silo.

We stared at the beautiful scene in front of us. It was like something out of a Norman Rockwell painting. In fact, I remembered how the designers at Q2 often used famous works of art or locations as inspiration for settings in different levels, so it very well could have been one of Rockwell's worlds. The only giveaway that we had left Earth was the dual suns, which stood a quarter turn apart from each other in the sky. That was one of *Kingdom*'s distinguishing characteristics across every level, but to witness it in person was simultaneously breathtaking and unnerving.

Rachel sat up. "I feel like I'm dreaming. It's like normal, but different. You know?"

"Me too." Aside from being exhausted, I still felt like myself, but breathing felt different, like in a high altitude where the air is thin.

She pointed to movement behind a split-level fence to our left. "Are those chickens?"

I tried to laugh, but I broke into a long coughing fit. There was still too much dust and grain in my lungs. "I think so."

"How did we end up here? I mean, this is Level 7, isn't it? The country farm? But the machine was programmed to send us to the same coordinates as the test run, the desert plateau. Wasn't that what Charlie said?" She glanced around us. "This is definitely not the same place."

I explained how I'd seen the coordinates panel change when we'd hit the chamber wall in the scuffle after they shot Charlie. "We must have altered the destination. This silo must be another portal in the digital bridge."

I reached into my pocket, pulling out the memory stick that Charlie had handed me before we'd entered the Eden chamber. It was dirty, but still in one piece.

"How are we supposed to use that if we don't have the communicator?" Rachel asked.

I dusted it off with my hand. "I don't know, but we have to try." I pulled my pants leg up and glanced at the ankle tracker. "We need to get these off too."

Rachel nodded, but then broke into a long, dry, hacking cough. "I need some water."

I stood and stared at the surrounding landscape. "We both need to drink something. We've breathed in too much dust." I pointed at the farmhouse. "That looks like as good a place to start as any."

"How does this even work?" asked Rachel, as we strode across the field, tall stalks of waist-high grass bending with our steps.

"What do you mean?"

"Are we real, or just electronic signals inside someone's computer? Is this really wheat, or is it just our imagination?" She reached out and brushed the tops of the stalks, the chaff crumbling at her touch. "It's too much to get my mind around."

I stopped at the edge of the yard in front of the farmhouse and listened.

"What if someone's in there?" Rachel whispered. "I mean, do people actually live here? Or are we alone in this virtual world?"

"We're about to find out."

We stepped onto the wide porch that wrapped around two sides of the farmhouse. A wooden swing with comfy-looking pillows hung from the ceiling on metal chains, and lush baskets of colorful flowers and green ferns lined the railings. A gentle breeze blew in from the fields, creating the ideal temperature for a lazy Sunday afternoon nap. It was like a place my mom had described from her childhood on a farm in Missouri. It was almost too perfect to be real, and I guess it was.

I pulled back a wood-framed screen door. The main door was already open, so we stepped into a square, high-ceilinged kitchen. Rachel found glasses in the cabinets and we both eagerly gulped down two glassfuls of cold water from the tap at the sink. Water had never tasted so good.

We were hesitant to call out, but it seemed clear that no one else was around aside from the animals we'd seen in the barnyard and the fields. It all just somehow existed. It was a farm that just worked with no human intervention. A benefit of life in a virtual world, I supposed.

We sat in the swing on the porch. I suddenly felt sleepy.

"I keep thinking about Charlie," said Rachel, her eyes set on mountains in the distance.

"Yeah, me too."

"What do you think happened to him?"

I put my hand over Rachel's. "You know what happened."

"Maybe he made it. We don't know where they hit him."

I nodded. "Maybe."

She turned and faced me. "He saved us, Bryce. I mean, I know he betrayed us, but he wanted to do the right thing in the end. Don't you think?"

"Yes. And he did, in the end."

A tear rolled down her cheek. "I hate it. All of it. I wish I'd never responded to that damn message! It's like a nightmare."

I put my arm around her shoulder. The truth was, I felt the same way, but I refused to let my mind go there. We had to keep fighting. If we gave up now, there was no return. Maybe the end result would be the same even if we fought, but I had to hold out hope.

We had to keep trying.

CHAPTER THIRTY-THREE_

I hadn't intended to fall asleep, but it was impossible not to in the odd warmth of the afternoon suns and the gentle breezes that moved across the porch. When I opened my eyes, the light was low in the sky and long shadows from the barn inched toward us across the grass. Rachel was stretched across my lap, her head resting on a cushion. I shifted my weight on the swing, my right leg half-numb from sitting too long in the same position.

Rachel stirred at the movement. She blinked her eyes and stared up at me, and for a moment, I felt a familiar contentment like when sitting with Maggie. I forced my mind to remember Rachel wasn't my girlfriend. But I couldn't deny that despite our relatively short time together, Rachel and I had bonded through our shared traumatic experience.

"Hey," Rachel moaned, stretching her arms and sitting up next to me. "Did you sleep?"

"Yeah. I must have been tired." She ran her fingers through her hair and stared out across the fields. "I just realized, I'm not hungry. Are you?"

I shook my head and glanced at the kitchen. "Not really, but if there was a homemade apple pie sitting on that windowsill, I think I'd still want to eat it."

"Maybe that's how it works here. We don't need to eat but we can for pleasure." She giggled. "Wouldn't that be great if it worked that way back home?"

"Fitz would like it."

Rachel's smile faded. "Sorry," I said, knowing I shouldn't have brought up such a negative subject.

She let out a long sigh and slid off the swing. "It's okay. Pretending doesn't change anything. This isn't a bed-and-breakfast. We're not on vacation." She turned back to me with determination in her eyes. "We have to keep moving."

She was right. I joined her at the porch railing. "We only have five hours until they recharge Eden. We need to find that communicator and upload the virus before they can make another transmission."

"But it's in the desert."

"Maybe we can change levels, just like when playing *Kingdom*."

Rachel pointed to the mountains beyond the fields. "What do you think's over there? Could the levels run into each other on a linear plane?"

I stepped down into the grass. "There's only one way to find out."

I expected her to follow, but I turned around to see Rachel still on the top porch step. She was staring over my shoulder at the old barn. "What's wrong?"

"Shh," she whispered. "Do you hear that?"

A faint noise was coming from the wooden structure. It

sounded electronic, like static and voices. Rachel jumped down the steps. "Come on."

Green ivy covered the entire left side of the wooden barn, its paint long gone. The back corner was missing as many boards as it held. A flimsy side door creaked loudly as I eased it open. Inside, streaks of shadows and light came and went through the cracks in the boards. I stepped forward, but a burst of motion exploded in the doorway. It rose from the ground and shot straight between Rachel and me. Rachel screamed, and I leaped back as a chicken flurried past us into the barnyard.

"Careful," I called nervously.

I stepped forward into the barn, wary of other flying shadows. We followed the steady static, like an old car radio whose station wasn't coming in clearly. If another person was in the barn, Rachel's scream would have announced our presence. But as we stepped toward the noise, there was no one else. I realized the static was coming from above our heads. I pointed to a ladder for the hayloft. The old wooden steps groaned under my weight, but they held as I rose toward the ceiling.

I poked my head into the loft. The sound flowed from the back of the space over piles of hay. I pulled Rachel up behind me, and we followed the sound to a cluttered old workbench on the far wall. The flat surface wasn't filled with tools and farm equipment, as might be expected, but with old electronic equipment—antique hand radios and speakers like some from World War II I'd seen in a museum.

Rachel wiped her finger along the equipment, years of dust gathering on her hand. "How did this get here?"

"No idea," I answered. "Maybe every level has its own portal. Each of them would need an access panel, right?"

"I guess that makes sense."

I remembered the memory stick in my pocket, but knew these old electronics would never be compatible. We tracked the source of the static to one of the radios. Somehow it was running, despite no evidence of a power source or electrical wires. I tried to adjust the dials. Alternating noises filtered in and out of the static, but they weren't much more than squeaks and squelches.

"Wait, go back!" said Rachel, listening closely.

I inched the knob to the left, and a garble of sound filtered through the speaker.

"There," said Rachel, moving closer. "Listen."

I turned a second knob, which seemed to be used for fine-tuning. Gradually, the noises became clearer. Someone was speaking between the static, rhythmically, repeating the same words over and over. What was he saying?

Rachel crouched down to the speaker, as I continued to fine-tune the transmission. Finally, the static subsided. It was a message on a loop.

You cannot run away. We are coming for you.

You cannot run away. We are coming for you.

You cannot run away. We are coming for you.

A shiver ran down my spine as I recognized the voice.

It was Yao.

CHAPTER THIRTY-FOUR_

Rachel lunged at the radio, her eyes ablaze. "I'm going to kill him!" She ripped the speaker from the desk and flung it across the hayloft before she sank to her knees and sobbed.

"It's not him, Rach. It's just a message."

She shook her head. "It's never going to end, is it?"

I pursed my lips. I didn't have an answer. But a glowing green light caught my eye. I bent down and crawled under the workbench toward a shiny, silver object that looked completely out of place in the rickety old barn.

"What is it?" Rachel asked.

"Oh my god," I gasped. It was a computer.

Rachel huddled next to me on the floor. "How is that possible?"

I moved closer to inspect the modern desktop terminal, which was just like those in Fitz's lab. It glowed with power, even without a visible power source. Maybe things didn't work the same in this world after all. I stood and pulled back a pile of burlap sacks on the corner of the table to reveal a monitor and keyboard.

I felt that glimmer of hope once more. Maybe there was still time.

We turned two empty wooden crates on their ends and positioned them next to the table like chairs at a workstation. I punched at the keyboard. Electronics flickered. The monitor flashed on.

"You thought the old radios were access points for the portal," said Rachel, "but maybe it's this computer." She stared at the glowing screen. "Can we use this to communicate to Tyler and Hendrickson? Could it upload the virus into Eden's mainframe?"

"We can try," I said, attempting to gauge whether we'd been gone more than five hours. "It's probably too much to ask to have a regular Internet browser on here."

"How would that even work, anyhow?"

I turned and stared at her. "How does any of this work, Rachel? If you hadn't noticed, I'm figuring this out as I go."

She crossed her arms. "Excuse me. I think we're both figuring things out, thank you very much."

I held up my hand. "You know what I meant."

"You're right. I'm sorry. There's no need for us to argue." She pointed at the keyboard. "Can I try?"

"Have at it." We switched seats, and I watched her pull up a simple coding interface menu. "What are you thinking?"

Rachel pointed at the screen. "If we hack into a simple source code file, we might be able to get a message to Tyler over the basic drop server I used to send him code. But I have no idea if it will work."

She typed a simple two-sentence message to Tyler,

explaining what level we were in, and that we needed help. But as she opened new windows, they began disappearing almost immediately. "What the hell?"

"Stop," I said. "They're tracking you."

"How?"

"I don't know, but now they can see which level we're in!"

"Can they do that?"

"Beats me, but we have to insert the virus now, before they shut the whole system down."

"Did I just give away our position?" Rachel moaned. "I don't even think the message went through to Tyler."

I crawled under the table with the memory stick in my hand. "There's no way to know if the message got out, but if they could sense you in the system, this must feed into their mainframe. If we can upload the virus before they lock us out, it just might work."

It was hard to see under the table, but thankfully the access panel ports were arranged like on the computers in the lab. I turned the drive stick and slid its narrow connector into an open slot.

"It's in!" I called up to Rachel. "Look for an execute file."

"I see it," she answered, "I'm opening the port icon…"

I stood next to her as she worked.

"Running the menus… there it is… external memory device… I found it!" She clicked on the virus file, and a message appeared asking if we wanted to execute.

Rachel glanced at me expectantly, and I nodded. "Do it."

She clicked *execute*, and the virus file upload streamed across the screen. We held our breaths, unsure of what would happen now. *Upload complete*, a message box declared in less than a minute.

Instantly, the screen flashed and then went dark. The terminal below the table seemed to shut off. "I think they closed us down."

"Did it work?" Rachel asked.

"I don't know," I answered, still staring at the screen. "It's not like we can try to access the Eden Machine from here. We can only hope that the virus infiltrates the mainframe and slows them down. That's what Tyler told me it would do in the first place, that it would stall their efforts long enough for JOSHUA to get operational."

"So now we wait?"

"Now we wait." I peered through a gap in the side of the barn. The suns were nearly set. "I'd still like to find the communicator and reach Tyler, but it'll be dark soon. We should wait until morning. There are beds in the farmhouse that are probably quite comfortable."

"But what if Tyler tries to contact us?" Rachel said. "We won't be able to hear."

I looked at the dark computer. "I don't know if that's usable anymore."

Rachel put her hands on her hips. "You never know. If they *did* get my message, I don't want to miss their reply."

I glanced at the bales of hay further into the loft. "You can use the house. I'll stay out here in the barn and listen for the radio."

Rachel shook her head. "I'm not sleeping in that house alone. Forget it."

"Then what?"

"We'll both sleep out here. We can bring out some blankets. But I'm not spending my first night in an alternate dimension by myself. There's no telling what happens here in the dark."

It was eerie walking through the deserted farmhouse at dusk. There were pictures on the walls of presumably fake people, every detail designed by programmers like us back at Q2. Maybe they'd used actual images of people that worked there, but who knew. It looked like none of the furniture had ever been sat on or slept in, which added to the creepy vibe.

I found two large backpacks in the farmhouse like ones Dad, Zach, and I used for camping. We loaded each pack with flashlights, matches, water bottles, and some cloth for bandages.

"What do you think?" Rachel came around the corner holding a pruning pole with a sharp folding saw on the end.

"For protection?"

"Sure, but also this." She pointed to the tracking device on her ankle. "Think it will cut it?"

I grimaced, but nodded. "We can try. Are you sure you're up for it?"

"We can't give them any further ways to track us. Who knows what information this thing is sending back. It needs to go."

She was right, and we agreed to try to cut her device first. I knelt on the floor while she propped her leg up on a kitchen chair. I prayed that blade was sharp enough.

Rachel let out a laugh. "Just don't slip."

"Don't move," I said as I carefully made a first pass. The metal blade cut a shallow groove into the plastic. It seemed to be working. A dozen more cuts, and the anklet fell to the floor. I breathed a sigh of relief when Rachel's leg didn't fall with it.

"And not a trace of blood," she said. "Are you sure you're not a surgeon?"

"Hardly."

She grinned at me. "Now the really hard part. Do you trust me as much as I trusted you?"

"Might as well get it over with." We switched positions, and I tried not picture the blade cutting into my flesh.

In about the same time as it took me, Rachel expertly cut through the plastic and the tracker was off. I scratched my leg, which felt itchy and bare after being covered so long. We smashed the trackers with rocks out in the yard.

I'd hoped the farm might be outfitted with an armory in addition to the access station, but the best I could find were the flashlights. The rest of the farm equipment—pitchforks, saws, and shovels—seemed too clunky and dangerous to carry around. The pruning pole could make a spear in a pinch, and I handed Rachel a steak knife from the kitchen. It seemed like we should both have something at the ready, just in case. We placed the packs on the porch swing, so we could grab them before heading out.

"It's getting dark," I said, pointing out the window. "We should get settled out there."

We carried several quilts and pillows out to the barn and spread them over bales of hay to form beds on each side of the loft.

"It looks great," said Rachel, "but there's one problem."

"What?"

"I'm not tired."

I laughed. "Me neither." I grabbed an extra quilt and pointed to the front of the loft. "Follow me."

We climbed over hay bales to a square window beneath a

slanted peak in the front of the barn. I spread the quilt across the opening so we would have somewhere to sit and hang our feet over the edge, creating a perch to watch the evening fade into night. I'd done it naturally, but now a twinge of guilt flooded through me. It was too much like the water tower.

Rachel seemed to sense something was bothering me. "What's wrong?"

I started to brush it off but then was honest. "This is a lot like a place I took Mags right before they took me."

"Mags?"

"Maggie."

"Was she the girl with you at the concert?"

I nodded. "She's a bigger London Towers fan than I am."

"I saw you two during the show, right before the encore. She's pretty." Rachel was silent for a moment. "Do you love her?"

I wasn't sure why I hesitated, but everything was so confusing. "Yeah, I think I do." I told Rachel about the pendant I'd made and how I'd placed the passcode on the back. "Now I wish I'd told her what it really meant."

"Do you think she'll show it to Hendrickson and Tyler?"

I shrugged. "How could she? She doesn't even know they exist."

Rachel stared at the now dark silhouettes of the mountains. The suns fell rapidly from the sky, in tandem, as if they were reflections of each other across the water. "Maybe she'll figure it out. We've been missing for a long time now. If I were them, I'd look for any small clue that could show where we'd gone."

"Maybe."

In just moments, the light had completely faded and billions of stars sparkled against an ebony sky.

"So weird," Rachel muttered.

"Yeah," I said, my head leaning far back, taking in the scene. "What about you?"

"Me?"

I chuckled. "Yeah, you. You had a date at the concert too. What was his name? Anthony?"

"Adam."

"Does he play *Kingdom*? Maybe he can break us out of here."

Rachel laughed. "No, he thinks video games are a waste of time."

"Sounds like Mags. So what's his deal?"

"He's a baseball player. He was drafted by Arizona out of high school last year. He's playing in A Ball in the minors this fall."

"Impressive."

"He thinks so." She giggled. "Did I say that out loud?"

"I won't tell anyone. You think he's the one?"

"Hmm… I don't really know yet. I mean, we've only been dating three months."

We sat silently for a time, listening to the night. "Do you really think the desert is over those mountains?" Rachel finally asked.

"Could be. I think we should get our packs from the porch in the morning and check it out. Exploring different areas could be helpful. We can use this farm as our base. It seems safe and has plenty of supplies. If the virus worked, they won't be able to come after us across the bridge. If it didn't, well…" I tried to think of something positive to say about that scenario, but couldn't find the words.

"I know, we're totally—" Rachel stopped mid-sentence.

A shiver ran through my body. Drumbeats, far in the distance, began a rhythmic pounding. I remembered them from playing *Kingdom* at home. Drums signaled that a hunting party or some other threat was near.

Rachel seemed to realize it too. She scooted back from the edge of the hay window. "I think I'm ready to go to sleep now."

We crawled back to the hay beds near the computer table. I tried to think positive thoughts. I didn't know who was out there, but I'd played enough rounds in the game to know it could be any number of dangerous things. Competing players would be armed for battle, totally unaware that we were real people and not just avatars. Rangers patrolled throughout the game, programmed to seek and destroy whatever was in their path. The country farm was normally a quieter training level, but now that we were here, nothing seemed safe. Night cats and other creatures were mostly found in the jungles and the mountain regions, so worrying about those could be left for another day.

I climbed between two quilts. The bed was stiff, but at least we had each brought a pillow. Rachel did the same in her bed. "You okay?" I called across the loft.

"Yeah."

"I'm sure it will quiet down soon." I turned over to find a comfortable position. "Good night."

"Night."

I lay listening to the drums, the ominous warning of what lay outside the wooden boards of the hay barn.

"Bryce?"

"Yeah?"

"Do you really think Charlie could have made it?"

I sighed and closed my eyes. "Maybe. I hope so."

"Me too. Goodnight."

"Goodnight."

I lay there for a long time, my head too filled with questions for sleep to come. When I'd nearly drifted off, a creak in the floorboards pulled me back awake. I froze until I heard quiet footsteps. Rachel dropped her pillow next to mine without a word. She lay above my quilt, but pressed her back against mine in the narrow bed.

For a long time, we lay there awake, silently listening to the drums. I think we both felt better having someone close, to not feel alone in this strange new world.

CHAPTER THIRTY-FIVE_

Light streamed onto the hay bales through the boards of the old barn. Rachel's arm draped over me, the crescent moon on her wrist turned up toward my face. My first reaction was to pull her closer. She looked beautiful sleeping there, and for an instant, I thought if we never got back home, I could be happy spending my days with her here in this strange place. But my brain quickly took over, and I gently lifted her arm and slipped out of the hay bed.

I left Rachel sleeping and climbed up to the hayloft window. A thin layer of fog glided over the pond, gradually lifting as the temperature rose. An empty rowboat lay on the shore. Two majestic swans paddled amongst the tall reeds that filled a narrow inlet, occasionally thrusting their long, white necks below the surface.

It was perfect. If only it were real.

Movement in the reeds drew my attention. The water rippled; maybe it was a family of ducklings paddling along. Then a larger figure stepped into view. It wasn't a duck. It was a person. I peered closer, surprised at the sight of a man fishing.

I instinctively took cover against the barn's rough boards. This was the first person we'd seen in the virtual world. Was he safe? Was he just scenery like the farmhouse, or an avatar that could guide us with directions? Was he dangerous?

I climbed over the hay bales to our bed in the back of the loft. "Rachel…" I whispered as I moved, "you won't believe it, but—" I stopped, realizing the bed was just an empty pile of quilts and pillows. Where had she gone?

I peeked through a crack in the boards on the side of the barn that faced the pond. I scanned for the fisherman, but stopped when I saw Rachel. She was walking directly toward the fisherman, who was waving to her from the pond.

I threw on my shoes and nearly slipped down the wooden ladder as I ran to catch up with her. Whoever or whatever that was in the pond, I didn't want her to face it alone. I caught up with her just as she reached the water. The fisherman, outfitted in tall wading boots, a vest, and a fly rod, was slowly trudging to the shore about thirty feet away.

"What do you think you're doing?" I asked, pulling at her arm.

Rachel turned in surprise, but smiled when she saw me. "Oh, hey. Look, it's a fisherman! He waved to me, and I thought he might be able to help us."

I squeezed her arm more tightly, pulling her next to the rowboat. "Wait. We don't know how this works. Or who he is."

The man had stepped onto the bank, his rod bouncing in the air as he walked toward us. It was too late now. We had no choice but to speak with him.

Rachel smiled and waved. "Good morning!"

The fisherman was about Dad's age, maybe a few years younger. He had sparkling blue eyes and a day-old stubble of dark beard with just a few specks of gray. He grinned at us from under his wide-brimmed hat. "Mornin'."

"Catch anything?" asked Rachel.

He nodded. "Couple o' bass, some perch. Not a lot at first, but they're startin' to bite. This is a good fishin' spot right here." His voice had a slight Southern twang. He turned and gazed across the valley. "Beautiful spot this time of the morning, isn't it?"

"Sure is," said Rachel.

I motioned to the farmhouse. "You live here?"

"Nah, just passin' through. How 'bout you folks?"

"Just visiting," replied Rachel.

"Beautiful spot," repeated the man, "this time of the morning."

Rachel nudged my side. "See," she whispered. "Just a coded avatar on a programmed interaction loop. I've seen them a hundred times playing the game. I don't think it's anything to worry about."

I tried to relax. Maybe she was right. I wouldn't last long if I stayed this wound up. I glanced at his fly rod. "Always wanted to learn how to do that."

The fisherman chuckled. "No time like the present, partner." He held it out. "Come on over and give it a whirl."

I glanced at Rachel, but she nodded.

"Why not?" I relented, stepping up to the water. Before handing me the rod, he demonstrated the proper technique for casting. He waved the rod back and forth gracefully, making the line dance through the air, before it rested on the water with barely a ripple. It looked easy, although I figured, like most things, it would be harder than it seemed.

He handed me the rod. "You try."

The pole felt light in my hands as I attempted the whipping action. But for me, the line came out just a bit and smacked at the water roughly. "I think it's going to take some practice," I said, turning to hand it back.

I dropped the rod at my feet.

The man had one arm around Rachel's waist, and the other brandished a wide hunting knife that he had pushed against her throat. "That's far enough," he growled.

"Bryce…" Rachel stood stiff against the knife blade.

"What are you doing?" I said, raising my palms. "Who are you? Let her go."

Behind him, two more men, dressed like soldiers, moved from the farmhouse to the barn. I should have known—Rangers. As a player in the game, you always had to be on guard. Rangers were ruthless, and the best of them could take out a player from a long distance. A trail of smoke drifted from the top window of the hay barn. Soon, flames were leaping through the boards, quickly engulfing the wooden structure. Across the barnyard, the grain silo where we'd come through the portal was also burning.

"You should have run farther away, children," said the man.

I didn't know if his appearance had changed or if my eyes were suddenly opened. Now I recognized him as a Ranger avatar in the game, a specialty character named the Sportsman, but a Ranger nonetheless. How could we have been so stupid?

If only I'd brought the pitchfork or the spear. The barn was in flames, and the farmhouse stood between us and the mountains, our only hope of escape. I wished the supply packs I'd assembled were closer than the porch. I spied two wooden oars lying inside the rowboat. That was something, at least.

My eyes met Rachel's, but she didn't seem panicked. Maybe with all we'd been through, we'd moved past being scared. Her glance bounced toward her waist. She was trying to tell me something. Her hand inched toward her pocket. I recognized the thin wooden handle of the steak knife I'd given her. Maybe she hadn't been so quick to trust after all.

A crash sounded in the barn as a section of the hayloft collapsed, spilling down into the lower rooms. For an instant, the Sportsman's attention was on the fire. We had an opening.

I reached for an oar as Rachel pulled the knife from her pocket. In a quick motion, she thrust it into the big man's leg. The Sportsman screamed out; whether he actually felt pain, I wasn't sure, but it distracted him enough to loosen his grip on Rachel. As she dropped to the ground, I swung the oar like an oversized baseball bat, catching him square in the head. He dropped like a stone, crumpling to the ground.

"Run!" I cried, grabbing Rachel's hand. I didn't know how long that would stop him, but we had to find cover in the woods.

When we reached the farmhouse, I broke our grasp and detoured onto the long porch.

"What are you doing?" Rachel cried.

"Keep going!" I called as I grabbed my backpack and then vaulted over the end railing and back to her in the grass. It had taken a few extra seconds, but at least we wouldn't be completely empty-handed in the mountains. The Sportsman was still on the ground, but the other two Rangers were now advancing toward us from the barn.

We leaped into the wheat field, the tall grass slowing our speed, but partially concealing us from the Rangers. I pointed ahead. "We have to make it to the trees!"

We sprinted with all our might. I was grateful to have the pack, but it was heavy. I knew I could maintain this speed for some time—the months of Coach Simmons' manic training program were paying off—but I didn't know how much endurance Rachel would have. She looked fit, but I could only hope that her adrenaline would carry her as far as the woods.

The field seemed to stretch forever. The woods grew closer, but we were slowing. Rachel stepped awkwardly then tumbled to the ground.

"My ankle," she moaned. "I twisted it in a hole back there."

"We have to keep going!" Sweat poured down my face. I looked back at the farm, but I couldn't see the Rangers. Were they following us? Was another squadron waiting at the edge of the field about to block our path? There was no way to know.

I leaned down and draped Rachel's arm over my shoulder. "Come on. We can't stop." We continued ahead, but our run had turned into a slow jog. With each step, Rachel winced in pain. But we were nearly to the trees. We just needed to go a little farther.

Suddenly Rachel stopped running. She turned to me, a pained expression covering her face. Half a second later, a piercing echo rang across the valley, that of a rifle shot ricocheting off the mountain range.

"No! Rachel!" I knelt and pulled her toward me. A red splotch was growing just below her shoulder.

"Bryce…" she pleaded, her breaths labored.

"Come on, hang in there, Rachel!" I glanced through the tall grass, but it was impossible to see anything from down on the ground. I tried to guess the distance to the trees. It wasn't far. We had no choice.

"I've got you," I said, hoisting her onto my shoulder and stumbling forward under the weight of both her and my pack. But I summoned my strength and powered forward. I could only hope that the tall grass obscured the Rangers' sights enough to lower their accuracy, but it was unlikely. I knew they were expert marksmen. I tried to weave back and forth as I took those final steps to the trees.

Two more yards. One more.

The tree to our left exploded just inches from my face as another shot echoed loudly. I surged forward, crashing into the undergrowth and deeper into the trees. We'd made it. For how long I didn't know, but we now had the chance to get away.

I set Rachel down gently on a large rock and pulled open her shirt, exposing her shoulder. Blood oozed from a dime-sized hole in her flesh. She looked up at me, her eyes distant.

"Sorry…" she said. "I should have known. I've always hated fishing."

"It's not your fault," I cried, pulling the bandaging cloth from my pack. I tore two long strips and wrapped them tightly around her shoulder. I prayed it would stop the bleeding. "Just hang in there." I pulled her up to her feet. "Can you walk? We have to keep moving."

Her face was pale, but she nodded. "I think so."

We moved slowly, stepping from tree to tree through the forest. We found a trail, which made walking easier, but we were moving uphill toward the mountains. The climb would have been tiring if we were at full strength, but it was nearly impossible with a gunshot wound.

We continued for almost an hour, but Rachel was moving slower and slower. Her strength was nearly gone. I knew we'd have to stop soon. There was no way I could carry her over the mountain. As we walked, I searched for somewhere we could hide—a ravine, a thicket, a cave. Then I saw a large rock outcropping. It could work. I thought there might be a cleft beneath the rocks, if not a full cave to provide cover and help us stay out of sight.

I pointed at the rocks. "Up here. We have to rest."

Rachel didn't argue. She looked like she was about to drop, so I reached down and scooped her into my arms. We moved up the rocks and away from the trail, stepping carefully down into a crevice. I hoped no creatures waited inside, but either way, I was prepared to fight. Nothing could be worse than what was chasing us.

I found a mossy space on the ground, three feet of clearance underneath a wide, silvery rock. I pulled off my sweatshirt and covered Rachel for warmth. The water canteen from my pack was full, but it wouldn't last long. I gently poured a few drops through her lips.

She swallowed and stared up at me. "Thanks."

"I'll be right back," I said.

"Promise?"

I nodded. "I just want to see if they're following." I grabbed the pruning rod, extending it into a five-foot pole and opening the blade at the top. It wasn't a rifle, but a spear was better than nothing. "You sit tight and hang in there." I took a long breath and tried to hold it together. I didn't want to think about her not making it. "Promise?" I added.

"Promise."

I stepped out, but she called me back. "Bryce?"

I leaned back into the cave.

"Be careful."

CHAPTER THIRTY-SIX_

I crawled out from beneath the rock overhang, making my way along the boulders that formed the top of the mountain. I stayed out of view from the path that cut back and forth to my right. I didn't want to stray too far from Rachel, but I had to see where we were. It was the only way I could make a plan for our escape from the Rangers.

At the summit, I caught my breath. The view was incredible. It hadn't seemed like we'd climbed so high up the mountain, but I could see in all directions. Behind me was the farm, resting peacefully in the valley. The only sign of distress was a faint tuft of smoke still rising from the ashen remains of the hay barn and silo.

I stared down between the mountains. There was a dip between the peak where I stood and its neighbor, just like back home where wind gaps often provided the route for highways to cut between a range. Our trail branched off just ahead and turned down into that dip, leading to a clearing. I squinted and saw a ring of stones around a dark, circular area. It took me a second to recognize it as a chasm, framed by the stones.

It was smaller than Grant's Gorge, the location where Zach and I would often play rounds back home on *Kingdom*, but it was the same idea.

Far in the distance, I saw the desert. The reddish glow of the canyons I'd seen on the wall screen back in Q2's lab reflected the dual suns. A long, wide plateau had been formed beside the canyon. It looked to be at least a day's journey, but we needed to find the communicator and attempt contact. There was no way to know if Rachel's message had made it through to Tyler and Hendrickson before we'd been shut down, or even if the virus had infiltrated the mainframe. But I suspected it had. If the bridge was still operational, someone would have come across by this point. It had certainly been over five hours. The Rangers who were after us were from within the game, not from back in our world.

Voices echoed to me from up the trail. They were closing in on us fast. I slid back, dropping into a wide, hollow tree that had fallen over behind the rocks. It was as big as an upended refrigerator, and I could easily fit inside. I silently watched the trail through a crack in the wood. Three Rangers came into view, spread in formation across the trail like they were a hunting party. The Sportsman was in the lead, but he had morphed into the image of a big game hunter, like he was tracking gazelle on the African savanna. He carried an enormous gun, and I saw no trace of the knife wound in his leg or where I'd clocked him with the oar.

I froze and listened.

"I know you're up here, Bryce." His voice bellowed, no longer folksy and friendly as he'd been by the pond. The sound was cold and rugged now. He'd stopped directly on the section of trail I could see, almost as if he knew where I was and was baiting me.

"We thought you might come quietly. Honorably. I'm sorry to see Rachel injured, truly I am. If you come now, we might be able to help her. Or is she already gone? Such a shame. She was a lovely girl and a bright programmer."

It was the Sportsman's voice, but the words he spoke were so familiar. It was Yao, speaking through the Ranger. I felt my blood pressure rise at the thought of him. Could he see me? Was he using the Ranger like a game piece, hunting for us through the levels?

"It was quite clever of you to upload the virus into our system. You might like to know that you were successful in disabling the bridge into *Kingdom*. An inconvenience to be sure, but fear not, it will be only temporary. A new team is already working on a fix.

"But I'm happy to report that the inbound bridge leading to our world is still fully functional. Mr. Fitz was able to wall off the path of the virus before it reached every aspect of the mainframe. There is more than one way to shake you out of hiding." He turned to the other Rangers. "Head down to the portal. I'm sure his family will be much more cooperative."

I watched the Sportsman turn and follow the other Rangers up the path and out of my view. Were they headed to the chasm? Was that the return portal? Why was he talking about my family? How did they have anything to do with this?

If the chasm was the return portal, then it could be our chance to get back home. We'd only just left, but this plan had gone all wrong. Charlie hadn't made it, we'd landed in the wrong location with no ability to communicate with Tyler, and now Rachel was seriously injured. The lab couldn't be much worse.

But first I had to get back to Rachel. I'd left her too long already. I knew the bullet had gone through her shoulder and she'd lost a lot of blood. I bounded down the peak, picking up the trail through the trees to the rock outcropping as soon as I felt it was safe. I stumbled twice in my hurry, sending a cascade of stones over the rocks, but I quickly regained my footing and continued on.

The sky was darkening. The clouds had formed into unnatural shapes that were outlined in a greenish glow. I couldn't tell if a storm was gathering or if it was the end of the world. I slid down to the rock crevice, ducking my head into the hiding place where I'd left Rachel. I said a silent prayer as I entered the space, not knowing what I'd find.

"Rachel?" I touched her face gently and then placed my head on her chest to listen for signs of life. She was breathing but barely responsive. I pulled my sweatshirt back and found it soaked in blood. This was bad.

"We have to get you out of here." I knew I should try to clean her wound. I knew she should rest, to avoid going into shock or bleeding to death, but I didn't think we had a choice. We had to get to the portal.

I started to explain my plan, but she was barely conscious and didn't seem to hear me. So I saved my breath, strapped on my pack, and then lifted her in my arms. Outside, the sky was ominously dark. As I stepped across the rocks toward the trail, a piercing roar filled the sky, sounding as if the heavens were ripping apart. A radiant green light shot through a hole in the clouds, streaming unnaturally down toward the chasm.

Despite her slender frame, Rachel seemed to grow heavier

with every step. I didn't know how long I could carry her, but I couldn't stop. I followed the Rangers' path toward the chasm. It was easier walking on the declining slope, but each time I glanced at Rachel's face, she looked to be slipping further away.

"Come on, Rach," I cried. "Just a little longer." I blinked back the tears, trying to clear my vision. If I tripped and dropped her on the trail, she might never get up. "I know you can stay with me. You have to keep trying."

Maybe she heard me, because right then she opened her eyes. She stared at the ghostly light filling the clouds. "The sky," she mumbled. "So much color…Bryce, what's happening?" She glanced at me, but then closed her eyes again.

I knew I needed to be cautious as I drew close to the chasm. Rangers would show no concern for Rachel's condition. They'd been the ones who'd shot her, and it was only dumb luck that they'd missed me.

I crouched behind a boulder at the top of a ridge. I had a clear view of the chasm now. The Rangers stood at the ring of stones, close to the chasm's edge, staring at the sky. The brilliant beam of light continued to inch its way to the ground, as if being pulled from the sky by the chasm's dark abyss. Even from my distance, I couldn't turn away from the pulsating green light.

When the beam met the ring of stones, the rocks seemed to suck in the light, suddenly sparkling like emeralds. A burst of energy shot in every direction. I could picture the Eden Machine reaching maximum speed, piercing through the dimensions. It was blinding, and I hid my eyes, overwhelmed without the dark goggles from the lab. I staggered back, but I held Rachel tight.

One by one, each Ranger stepped forward, dropping into the void. Did they fall into the depths, or was the bridge immediate? It didn't matter. There was no time. I struggled to my feet, hobbling across the clearing. The beam was still filling the chasm, but the intensity was already dispersing.

I ran faster. Rachel bounced in my arms. We had to make it. There was no other choice.

We were twenty feet from the stones. Ten. But with a final, giant burst of energy, the green pulse vanished in an instant, sucked into the chasm's depths. The forest turned eerily still. Only the stones continued to glow brightly.

I fell to my knees, cradling Rachel's unmoving body in my arms. I raised her head to listen for her breath, but she was gone. I was too late.

"No!" I screamed across the silence. Tears streamed down my face as I pulled her close, kissing her cheek.

It was over. They had won.

Whatever faint trace of hope that we had found—was gone.

CHAPTER THIRTY-SEVEN_

I sat in the clearing holding Rachel's body for a long time. Eventually I stood from the grass and stepped onto a stone. I stared into the chasm. Darkness. Endless depths of blackness. It might as well have been a mirror, reflecting my defeated heart. The portal was closed.

Despite our best efforts, the virus had only knocked out half of Eden's bridge. It was still more than capable of destroying all that I held dear. I tried not to imagine the Rangers storming into Milton, or what they might do to my parents, to Zach, or to Maggie.

For a moment, I considered taking one tiny step forward. That's all it would take to end my pain. This was likely the end for me anyhow, permanently lost here in this dangerous, artificial world. Falling to the depths would just speed up the end result.

I glanced back at Rachel. She looked so peaceful, lying in the grass, bathed in soft light from the sky, which had returned to normal. The suns were already beginning to slide toward the horizon. Nightfall had come quickly at the farm. I couldn't leave her for whatever creatures lurked in these woods during the night. She deserved so much more than that.

It was completely dark when I finished. Sweat soaked through my T-shirt. I'd used whatever I could find for the digging—the spear blade, flat rocks, even my hands. It was a shallow grave, but I felt like I owed Rachel that small amount of dignity. I fashioned some rounded stones into a crude pattern of a crescent moon to match the tattoo on her wrist. She'd never shared why she had that marking, but it was a piece of her, and the stones were lasting evidence that she had existed in this horrid world.

When the last stone was placed, I organized my remaining supplies in the pack and tried to clear my mind for the task ahead. It was foolish to trek onward in the dark, but I didn't care. Too much had happened. I had to send a warning that danger was coming. If I could reach my family, perhaps they could get to Tyler or Hendrickson. They were now our only hope.

Beyond the thick forest lay the desert. From the mountain peak, I'd seen the long, flat plateau in the distance. It would likely take a day or more to get there, but I had to reach the communicator. If there was any chance for me at all, it lay there. I followed the trail in that direction, away from the farm and the chasm. Away from my memories of Rachel, and toward the desert plateau.

* * *

I WAS LUCKY. Billions of stars lit the night sky, a mesmerizing display that allowed me to see the wide trail. I held the flash-light I'd taken from the farmhouse, but kept it dark. It might draw attention, something I was desperate to avoid. Rangers or creatures that I preferred not to name could be lurking in these woods.

It felt different without Rachel. I was now a lone traveler in a foreign world. Perhaps this was what the early explorers had felt—Columbus, Magellan, John Smith, or even Neil Armstrong on the surface of the moon. Had they also felt scared and alone? How did they continue on? Were they fueled by their dogged determination to succeed, or did a refusal to fail drive them forward? Maybe there was no difference.

I'd walked for hours, and the miles of dense forest were now thick like a jungle along the Amazon. This level hummed with life on every side. Hoots and hollers, wild screams and roars all cascaded from the tops of the trees. It echoed through the undergrowth, as if someone had warned the inhabitants of these woods that a trespasser loomed near. An alien was among them.

The edges of the trail seemed to grow closer, filled with sounds of scurrying feet and scraping claws. The branches and leaves that draped across the trail above me were bouncing and shaking with movement. Seedpods and round fruit the size of oranges dropped down like rain. It was like walking through a zoo with all the fences lowered, except I was the attraction, and the creatures in the darkness were the spectators.

The leaves along the trail fluttered, as though from the breath of some unknown being, and I couldn't shake the feeling that something was creeping nearer. I wished I had one of the Ranger's heavy guns and not just a flashlight and homemade spear. I tensed, waiting for a confrontation.

It finally came with a scream—a terrifying roar that rattled down my spine. Only one creature in *Kingdom* made that sound. In the polar regions, it presented as a snow leopard, in the desert, as a tanned mountain lion, but in the forests and jungles, where I had unwisely ventured, it was the night cat—a deadly panther with claws the size of switchblades and teeth like ice picks. Aside from the Rangers, it was the fiercest obstacle that roamed between levels.

The first scream came from my left, but in an instant, it was at my [illegible]. It was circling me, stalking me—I had been identified as prey.

I clutched the spear tightly but continued forward. I shined my light ahead where the path dipped into a shallow gully before rising to the next ridge. On each side of the trail were sheer rock cliffs, like where they had blasted a route through the mountain for the highway back home. I gulped, recalling spots like this I'd seen when playing the game. This was a kill zone, a natural trap where a predator could easily strike.

I didn't run, fearing it would only speed the attack. Each step forward was a step closer to reaching the edge of the jungle and the desert plateau. If only I could get past this gully.

I flashed my light to the top of the ridge. Two ghostly, yellow-green eyes reflected in the beam. The night cat's lips curled back into a snarl, its deadly fangs glistening like sabers.

I could barely breathe as the eyes watched me from the ridge. I gripped the flashlight in my left hand, my spear in my right, but they would be no match for the cat. I realized that after all that had happened, this was how it would end. Not with the quick bullet of a Ranger's gun, but torn to shreds by this savage beast.

The deadly cat crept forward. I had no choice but to abandon the trail, bolting for the trees ahead of the rock formations. I climbed up the back of the incline that formed the cliff beside the trail. I heard the beast chasing me, darting gracefully between the trees, closing the distance. I paused twenty feet from the edge of the cliff on my left. I searched for a tree to climb or a crevice I could crawl into that would be out of the cat's reach, but the tree branches started far above my head and leaves evenly covered the ground.

The cat stopped behind me on the crest of the hill. It knew I was trapped. I must have seemed amusing to the beast, gripping my small light and knife-capped pole. I waved my spear at the cat, but the pole knocked against a tree trunk and the weapon fell from my hands. The cat crouched, motionless, twenty feet away, ready to pounce. I glanced back at the edge of the cliff that was just past two thick tree trunks standing three feet apart. I could jump to my doom or be ripped apart limb from limb. One last thought came to my mind.

I bent down and slowly picked up the spear. Then, with a crazed shout, I launched my flashlight at the yellow eyes. The night cat screamed, enraged at my nerve, but I used the distraction to lunge toward the cliff. From the corner of my eye, I saw the cat take three quick steps and then leap into the air. I could almost feel its breath on my neck as I dropped to the ground, sliding through the leaves and between the two tree trunks. With both hands, I gripped the spear pole, turning it horizontal to the ground. Each end of the pole caught against a tree, stopping my body's slide at the edge of the cliff. The screaming cat flew past, its razor claws just inches from my face. It soared between the trees and over the edge of the precipice.

I waited for another scream, but the forest was still. The flurry of activity in the woods was suddenly silent, as if shaken by the fall of the mighty predator. I lay shaking in the leaves. Finally, I released my grip on the spear and slowly rose to retrieve my flashlight. I stepped over to the edge. The dark outline of the defeated cat was spread across the trail fifty feet below.

CHAPTER THIRTY-EIGHT_

Dawn finally broke as I exited the jungle. The new level of the central plateau rose in the distance. Rachel seemed to have been correct that the levels ran consecutively together. As familiar as *Kingdom* was to me, everything felt different from my perspective on the ground. I pressed forward as the suns rose through the sky. At their midpoint, I started up the cliff, climbing toward the flat expanse I knew lay at the summit.

A final handhold, one last push, and my head broke above the plateau. A low-forming cloud hung just feet above me, creating an odd shadow against the hard, flat rock. It felt like a soft comforter tucking me into a bed. I peered across the wide desert. The light bent at odd angles through the clouds, but I saw the unmistakable boulder in the center, wavering like a mirage in the heat. I'd seen it on the screen in Fitz's lab, an enormous stone in the center of the plateau, placed like a centerpiece on a long banquet table.

I started to run, my spirits strengthened by finally reaching my destination. The communicator sat near the base of the boulder, like it had been there for centuries. It was incredible, seeing something that had been back in the lab and now placed in the virtual world. I kneeled beside the machine. I'd been working a plan through in my mind most of the morning, but I could only plan so far without seeing the device up close. As much as I had hoped the communicator would serve my purposes, my idea was only theoretical. Now that I had arrived, fear ripped through me that my plan or the machine might not work.

The cloud quickly dispersed, but it was replaced by a scorching heat. Could my skin could burn here, perched under not one but two suns on the giant griddle of the plateau? With the cloud cover gone, I'd also be easy game for an attack or a Ranger's long-range rifle.

The men in the lab had carried the communicator, but I found that it also had wheels. I unlocked each corner and then pushed the device the dozen yards to the base of the boulder. I remembered thinking the towering rock had looked like a capital letter T when I'd seen it on the monitor in the lab. But now standing next to it, I noticed an opening under the crossbar. I wheeled the communicator through a wide cleft in the rock to a small cave. The space was not much bigger than the bathroom Zach and I shared back home, but it would be enough to keep me protected and hidden while I worked on the machine.

To my amazement, the communicator started up without any electrical hookup. Maybe it used rechargeable solar batteries. That could explain why they'd selected this location in the desert. But the computer in the hay barn had also operated without an obvious power source. Perhaps everything in this world was powered automatically, as if the current flowed through the atmosphere like oxygen did on Earth. It would be a tech company's dream come true.

I contemplated whether Yao's people could shut the communicator down as quickly as they killed the computer at the farm. It would be useless for me to activate the device only to have it immediately compromised. According to Charlie, Q2 had sent the device to this location to be a base for all communications between worlds and I doubted they would risk destroying it. Their designs for this project stretched far beyond my measly existence.

I scrolled through the interface for several hours and learned that the terminal had partial access to the mainframe, video recording capabilities, and contained sections of *Kingdom*'s source code. The last part was a mind-bender, since I was inside of the game. While not a gaming console, it accessed areas of the code that could create small alterations to the program. I knew I could use that to my advantage.

I had hoped to contact Tyler and Dr. Hendrickson, but the communicator seemed limited to the Eden Machine, which I'd partially disabled, and things on the *Kingdom* side of the digital bridge. I found, however, that I could make small alterations—plant a tree, form a cave inside a canyon wall, or develop a simple avatar. I tried to add a useful weapons cache or a transport vehicle, but that was restricted.

My mind wandered through the possible uses of these functions like I was developing a coding sequence. I may not be able to get back home, but what if I could lure someone from home to me? Not physically bringing them across the bridge, but virtually, guiding them from inside the game? I knew Zach played *Kingdom* religiously. I doubted he'd abandoned the habit since I'd been gone, however long that was. A message to him in *Kingdom* would work nearly as effectively as a message to him back home in Milton.

But I had to be discreet. Zach had played under the username *ZFlyer97b* for years. A direct message would only put a target on his head, if there wasn't one already. Q2 would see something like that in minutes. I would have to create a back door that he would recognize on his own. But there wasn't much time. I had to move quickly.

I positioned the communicator across the tight space of the cave, pointing my flashlight beam like a spotlight. I pressed *record* and then crouched down along the wall into the light and the view of the camera.

"Hey, Zach," I began. "Yes, it's really me."

CHAPTER THIRTY-NINE_

After recording the message to Zach, I broke down in tears. Speaking to my little brother when I was so far from home had been harder than I'd expected. My body was drained, but I pulled myself back to the communicator and uploaded the message into the mainframe. If Zach could get Maggie's pendant to Tyler and Hendrickson, it should enable the cooling sequence for their quantum accelerators. It would be the final piece to get the JOSHUA machine operational.

I routed the video to be waiting for Zach in a cave sequence. The password logic from our trapdoor game secured access. I considered how to best lead Zach to the cave in the canyon wall. An avatar of me was too risky. It would quickly draw attention from Q2 or even other game players. It needed to be something inconspicuous.

I thought back to when I had been waiting for Tyler at the overlook. A fox had sat and watched me across the parking lot, as if he knew what was happening and had wanted to lead me to the truth. It could work.

A sound interrupted my thoughts. A slow, rhythmic

thumping. As the files completed their sync onto the mainframe, I crept out to the entrance of the rock formation. Night had fallen over the plateau. A cold, biting wind had picked up outside the protected confines of my cave. Was this a normal weather pattern across the flat plateau, or had something sensed my presence and whipped up the elements to drive me away? I stepped away from the rock and was immediately pelted by sand. I lifted my arm across my face, squinted my eyes, and listened. The thumping still sounded above the wind's roar. Someone was coming.

I ran back into the protection of the cave for one last piece of the puzzle. I searched the mainframe directories, praying that our group competition program would still be there and that I'd have access. My hunch was that they wouldn't have secured it. They would never have envisioned this situation—me alone across the digital bridge, attempting to hack their orientation files.

I opened a promising-looking folder and held my breath. Our hologram program. I copied the files to the communicator and hoped that what Charlie, Rachel, and I had built in those early days at orientation would work. I wanted one more way to attract Zach's attention. I needed to play every chip I had to win this crazy game.

While the fox avatar copied into the hologram application, I considered the best location back home to place it. A fox roaming across our front lawn or in our living room would be too much. Mom and Dad might call the police. I needed somewhere that Zach was sure to find it, so that when he saw the fox again in *Kingdom*, he would know it was meant for him. The field between Maggie's neighborhood and ours would be just the thing. Zach cut through behind the Harpers' house to get to the bus stop every day.

I stared at the communicator as the final file executed. Now I just had to wait for Zach to find my breadcrumbs and pray that it all avoided detection by Q2. It was a lot to ask. Zach would have to reach Tyler and Hendrickson, evade any Rangers that might come for him, and perhaps the biggest question mark, the passcode on Maggie's necklace would have to unlock the missing components to make the JOSHUA machine operational.

Maybe it was *too* much to ask, but it was all I had left. I leaned my head against the hard wall of the cave. I'd been up and moving for nearly two days. I was exhausted. Waking up in the hayloft with Rachel seemed like weeks ago.

The drums were still pounding, but they didn't seem to grow closer. I closed my eyes. If I could get a little rest, I just might make it.

CHAPTER FORTY_

I left the plateau at dawn. The winds had subsided, but the searing heat had returned. I wrapped my head with a wide strip of the remaining bandage cloth to keep the sun off my face. This side of the plateau was longer than where I'd entered, but I stumbled on. It was only a matter of time before Q2 placed guards around the communicator, and I didn't want to be in the cave when they showed up. I had to keep moving and find a hiding place. I couldn't return to the jungle, it was far too dangerous, and the plateau was too hot. I hoped the canyon would be more hospitable.

When I reached the edge of the plateau, I carefully climbed down the sharp cliff. I rested at the bottom, but soon set off into the canyon. The entire area appeared to be a dry creek bed, perhaps once a raging river, like the Colorado that cut through the bottom of the Grand Canyon. I laughed out loud at the thought, since this place had no history. It had not been around for millennia like my world. The canyon, the two red suns, the plateau—they were all man-made, figments of a programmer's wild imagination. It was hard to fathom even after experiencing it first-hand.

The branches caught my attention first, waving from the top of a palm tree in a gentle breeze. I thought it must be a mirage—the suns playing tricks on me after too many hours of wandering. But I moved closer, led onward by my thin thread of hope. The palm was accompanied by several smaller trees, some bushes, and grass—all green and lush. A shallow pool had formed from a thin stream flowing out of the rock. I bent down and splashed cool water on my face. It wasn't a mirage—it was an oasis.

Sometimes it's the small things that can rejuvenate us the most. They keep us going even when our prospects are bleak. That oasis renewed my hope. Virtual or not, I was so thankful for whatever programmer had included it in the desert level. I guarantee they did not have me in mind when they coded it, but it would make the perfect place to hide. It became my base, a place I could return to each day after scouting the region in my never-ending quest to find a way home.

I don't know for sure how long I lived there. It felt like several weeks, but I stopped counting after a handful of days. It wasn't clear if time was the same here inside *Kingdom* as it was back home. Maybe a day here was equal to a month on Earth, or maybe it was the other way around. There was no way of knowing.

I feared leaving the desert level, since I didn't want to stray too far from the communicator. It was my sole connection to the real world. I'd returned twice, always traveling under the cover of darkness, searching the mainframe for any loopholes I had previously missed or any sign that my video had reached Zach. But there was nothing.

On other days, I explored deeper into the canyon. It seemed to stretch on for miles, but I never found another oasis. The only place of significance I discovered was a large cave far up the canyon wall. Inside was a deep pool with water that turned green in the sunlight streaming through a round opening in the ceiling. That was how I had found the cave, I'd been climbing along the rocks and nearly tumbled through the hole above the pool. Eventually I'd found a passage that led to the floor inside, and twice I'd rested by the quiet water to escape the desert heat.

I was afraid to build anything at my oasis that might draw attention. I'd crafted a simple bed with grass and palm branches, and each morning, I filled my canteen from the clear, narrow stream that trickled from the canyon wall. I never got particularly hungry, but one of the smaller trees in the oasis produced a golf-ball-sized red fruit that tasted like watermelon and smelled like roses. Clearly another product of a creative coder's imagination.

There was some evidence of life in the canyon. A random animal occasionally crossed my path—I saw jackrabbits, deer, squirrels, and other rodents. Once I saw a fox, but I knew right away it wasn't mine. Each was just a simple avatar, and they all kept to themselves. Many nights I heard the drums, thumping in the distance. Only once did other players enter the canyon. Their torches lit up the tall rock walls like ghosts. But my oasis was far enough off the main trail that they hadn't turned in my direction. I knew there were more deadly concerns, even in the desert—cougars, rattlesnakes, scorpions, and of course Rangers—but they'd been strangely absent since I'd arrived.

Each night, I dreamed of home—my family, Maggie, but

also of Charlie and Rachel. It pained me to remember that my teammates were both gone. I didn't know which of us had met the better fate. Their lives had been snuffed out far too soon, but mine was stuck in no-man's-land here across the bridge. Even though I'd known them both for just a short amount of time, they held a small corner of my heart.

I wouldn't have made it without that clump of green amidst the rocky landscape. My oasis kept my hope alive, even if just a speck. I had no choice but to trust that Yao's people had not yet fixed the Eden Machine, that my family was safe, that Zach had found my message and showed Maggie's code to Tyler and Hendrickson, and that the JOSHUA machine would be completed.

It was likely too much to ask, but I still dreamed that I might be saved.

CHAPTER FORTY-ONE_

I heard it before I saw it, which I suppose was the idea. The sound was unmistakable. I was scouting as usual across the canyon when the rattlesnake slithered out from behind a crack in the rock in front of me, a diamond-shaped pattern clearly visible despite the shadows cast from the gathering clouds in the sky. The snake's forked black tongue shot out from its triangle-shaped head, like it was testing the air. I couldn't remember if snakes had poor hearing or bad eyesight, but it seemed to know I was near. The tip of its tail was raised and rattled an ominous warning.

Was this another harmless scenery avatar, or a deadly obstacle like the night cat? I stepped carefully backward, keeping the coiled creature fully in my sights. There was no point in risking it. But another flash of motion caught my eye. A second snake slithered out from the sand on my right. Then another. I'd stumbled into a viper pit. I spun around, suddenly encircled by dozens of the venomous snakes, their tails all shaking wildly. Rattling noises filled the air like the sound of cicadas swarming the trees on a summer night.

I'd learned never to explore without my pack. I slowly retrieved the trusted spear pole. It had saved me once on the cliff with the night cat; perhaps it could do magic again. The snakes tightened the circle they'd formed around me, like a pack of wolves moving in. This wasn't natural behavior for rattlesnakes—they'd clearly been custom designed to attack. I waved the pole like a golf club, swinging wildly to keep the creatures back. I connected with two, severing one in half and sending the other hurling across the sand, but they were coming faster than I could drive them away. More snakes streamed from crevices in the rocks. Dozens of them. Hundreds maybe.

My desperate circumstances had distracted me from the growing darkness across the canyon. When I finally glanced up, I nearly dropped my spear. There was no mistaking that sky. I immediately recognized the eerie green glow and how the clouds mounted in fearsome formations like the heavens were marching off to war.

The snakes began scattering in all directions, retreating back into the rocks as if they knew what was about to happen. Then the sky ripped open, and the brilliant jet stream of light began pushing from the gap in the clouds. The bridge was opening.

At first I stood frozen, awe-struck, watching the event occur. It was what I'd longed for all those days and weeks, but now that it was happening, I couldn't move.

What did it mean? I'd been hiding alone and without anyone to talk to for so long, I couldn't think clearly. Had Yao defeated the virus and repaired the Eden Machine? Maybe it was Yao himself.

But there was another possibility—the JOSHUA machine

could be operational. Zach could have contacted Hendrickson and Tyler with the code from Maggie's pendant, or they might have just figured out what they needed to do on their own. They could be opening the return portal for me to get back home. I fought conflicting emotions, unsure whether to be thrilled or horrified.

The beam slowly crept toward the ground. Where was it landing? They'd destroyed the grain silo where Rachel and I had arrived. The Rangers had left from a portal at the chasm, but that was over a day's journey from the canyon, and the beam was tilting closer to where I stood. The plateau was the more likely target. If Yao was sending through an Eden transmission, it would probably be to the same spot he'd sent the communicator. But if Yao was opening the bridge, that would mean Zach and the others had failed.

I sank down into the sand. I couldn't run anymore. If Yao had fixed the bridge, there would be no reason to keep hiding. My demise was inevitable.

But something was off. The beam was aimed toward the desert, but the closer it came, the more the angle slanted away from the plateau. It was heading past me, deeper into the canyon. What did that mean? Hope spilled back into my mind. I leapt up and raced after the brilliant light like I was chasing the end of a rainbow.

My work surveying the canyon paid off as I expertly scrambled along the barely visible footholds in the rock. Halfway up the canyon wall, I realized where the beam was heading. The pool I had discovered in the cave. Could it operate as a portal just like the grain silo and the chasm? It had to. There was nothing else up this canyon wall.

I raced over the rock, desperate now, not caring what

danger was beaming toward me across the dimensions. If the pool was the portal, it could be my chance—my last chance—to get back home.

I headed directly for the opening in the rock above the pool. I had to shield my eyes as I crested the last ridge. The beam of light had touched down, radiating energy directly through the hole in the ceiling above the pool. I didn't have time to wind around to the cave's side passage. I'd have to leap into the jet stream from above the pool.

But as I prepared for my final spring into the opening, a burst of energy knocked me off my feet. A fantastic flash pulsed from the opening above the cave. Then everything was still.

I blinked. The jet stream was gone. The bridge had closed.

I was too late.

I stepped to the edge and looked down. The rocks still sparkled with a green hue from the intense burst of energy. I peered down through the natural skylight, realizing they hadn't opened the bridge to bring me home. They'd sent something across, into this world. Was it more equipment? A second communicator? Why had the bridge closed so quickly?

I strained to see into the cave. The water glowed with a phosphorescent light. Something moved in the green-tinted liquid, deep below the surface. Someone had crossed the bridge. The figure was too small to be a hulking Ranger. Was it a kid?

I jumped feet-first through the opening, dropping twenty feet into the pool like a rescue diver from a Coast Guard helicopter. The water was green, but clear. The sunlight allowed me to see easily when I opened my eyes underwater. I scanned all around me, then below, remembering how the pool was surprisingly deep. A body drifted listlessly, a mop of hair obscuring its face.

My head cracked the surface, and I pulled in a long breath before diving for the body. It was barely moving when I reached it. Recognition flashed through my brain, but there was no time to think about it. Just as I had with Rachel's body in the grain silo, I grasped the swimmer's body in my best rescue hold and kicked with all my might toward the surface. I'd nearly exhausted my air supply when we finally broke through the top of the water.

I dragged the body to the side of the cave. Alarm bells were screaming in my mind, but I refused to listen to them as I heaved the boy onto the rock. I pushed back the wet hair that was obscuring his face.

Then my breath disappeared. It couldn't be. This was all wrong.

I stared down at the familiar features.

It was Zach.

ACKNOWLEDGMENTS_

Some books are a tough go, but this one came together surprisingly quickly. It provided the perfect diversion between ideas for my next book in *The Virginia Mysteries* series. I knew there was so much more to tell about Bryce's story, and I was anxious to share how he got into such a mess with Final Kingdom, Q2, and Dr. Hendrickson.

Writing a semi-prequel can be tricky, since messing with the past can change the future. That's not a good idea when I already had *The Missing* completed. Creating a new world and backstory is fun, and getting to know Bryce, Charlie, Rachel, and the devious crew at Q2 was a blast. I hope my low-tech science ideas proved convincing enough to keep you moving through the story like it did for me. As I shared in the last book, the Final Kingdom series came about as an effort to write something that kids who loved video games (like my boys) would get into. Getting them to spend a few hours reading instead of in front of the screen, it would be a win-win. Like most of my books, this one turned out to be more about adventure than gaming, but I hope that broadens the audience and keeps things exciting for everyone.

Sending a new book out into the world is a big effort, and there is a long list of folks to thank—Mary, Aaron, Haley, Mom, and Gracie for their early reads and feedback, and Matthew and Josh for holding fast to their teenage determination to not read my recent books.

My publishing is a team makes life so much easier—editing by Kim Sheard, proofreading by Stephanie Parent, covers Dane at ebooklaunch.com, and my awesome advance reader team who help get early reviews out into the world to attract new readers.

Most importantly, thank you to my readers for your support and enthusiasm. After fifteen books, it's still exciting to push a new one out of the nest and see if it can fly. I hope there are many more to come.

ABOUT THE AUTHOR_

Steven K. Smith is the author of *The Virginia Mysteries*, *Brother Wars*, and *Final Kingdom* series for middle grade readers. He lives with his wife, three sons, and a golden retriever in Richmond, Virginia.

For more information, visit:

www.stevenksmith.net

steve@myboys3.com

ALSO BY STEVEN K. SMITH_

The Virginia Mysteries:

Summer of the Woods

Mystery on Church Hill

Ghosts of Belle Isle

Secret of the Staircase

Midnight at the Mansion

Shadows at Jamestown

Spies at Mount Vernon

Escape from Monticello

Pictures at the Protest

Brother Wars Series:

Brother Wars

Cabin Eleven

The Big Apple

Final Kingdom Trilogy (10+):

The Missing

The Recruit

The Bridge

DID YOU ENJOY THE RECRUIT?_

WOULD YOU … REVIEW?

Online reviews are crucial for indie authors like me. They help bring credibility and make books more discoverable by new readers. No matter where you purchased your book, if you could take a few moments and give an honest review at one of the following websites, I'd be so grateful.

Amazon.com
Goodreads.com

Thank you and thanks for reading!

Steve